MARVEL CINEMATIC UNIVERSE
PHASE TWO

MARVEL
ANT-MAN

MARVEL CINEMATIC UNIVERSE
PHASE TWO

MARVEL

ANT-MAN

Adapted by ALEX IRVINE

Based on the Screenplay by EDGAR WRIGHT &
JOE CORNISH and ADAM McKAY & PAUL RUDD

Story by EDGAR WRIGHT & JOE CORNISH

Produced by KEVIN FEIGE, P.G.A.

Directed by PEYTON REED

LITTLE, BROWN AND COMPANY
New York   Boston

marvelkids.com

This book is a work of fiction. Names, characters, places, and incidents are the product of the author's imagination or are used fictitiously. Any resemblance to actual events, locales, or persons, living or dead, is coincidental.

© 2016 MARVEL

Little, Brown and Company

Hachette Book Group
1290 Avenue of the Americas, New York, NY 10104
Visit us at lb-kids.com

Little, Brown and Company is a division of Hachette Book Group, Inc.
The Little, Brown name and logo are trademarks of Hachette Book Group, Inc.

The publisher is not responsible for websites (or their content) that are not owned by the publisher.

First Edition: April 2016

ISBN: 978-0-316-25638-4

10 9 8 7 6 5 4 3 2 1

RRD-C

Printed in the United States of America

PROLOGUE: 1989

Hank Pym strode into the large conference room deep inside the under-construction S.H.I.E.L.D. headquarters known as the Triskelion and saw Howard Stark, Mitchell Carson, and Peggy Carter deep in conversation, exactly where the guard outside had said they would be. "Stark," he snapped.

"He doesn't seem happy," Stark murmured.

Stark stood up to meet Pym. "Hello, Hank. You're supposed to be in Moscow."

"I took a detour through your defense lab," Pym said.

He got to the table and slapped down a steel-and-glass vial containing a red fluid.

"Tell me that isn't what I think it is," Carter said, turning to Stark.

"It depends if you think it's a poor attempt to replicate my work." Pym glared at the S.H.I.E.L.D. brain trust, furious at what they had done. He could see immediately that Carter hadn't known this sample existed. "Even for this group, that takes nerve."

"You were instructed to go to Russia," Carson said. "May I remind you, Dr. Pym, that you're a soldier—"

"I'm a scientist," Pym interrupted.

"Then act like one," Stark shot back. "The Pym Particle is the most revolutionary science ever developed. Help us put it to good use."

Pym couldn't believe what he was hearing. "First you turn me into your errand boy and now you try to steal my research?"

With a condescending smirk on his face, Carson said, "If only you'd protected Janet with such ferocity, Dr. Pym."

That was it. Pym lost his temper and punched Mitchell Carson square in the nose.

Peggy Carter grabbed his arm before he could throw another punch. "Easy, Hank."

"You mention my wife again and I'll show you ferocity," Pym growled.

Carson, grimacing, wiped blood away from his nose. He looked over at Stark, like he wanted him to take his side.

Stark wouldn't. "Don't look at me—you said it."

Pym couldn't work with these people. They were too tied up with the government and their secret plans. He'd been mistaken to start working with them in the first place. "I formally tender my resignation," he said.

Stark shook his head. "We don't accept it. Formally. Hank, we need you. The Pym Particle is a miracle. Please, don't let your past determine the future."

"As long as I am alive," Pym said very slowly, "nobody will ever get that formula."

He stalked out of the conference room, wishing he'd thrown that second punch.

"We shouldn't let him leave the building," Carson said. He was embarrassed and angry, and wanted to get back at Pym somehow.

"You've already lied to him; now you want to go to war with him?" Carter clearly didn't think it was a good idea. Carson was letting his emotions get the better of him.

"Yes," Carson growled. "Our scientists haven't come close to replicating his work."

"He just kicked your ass full-size," Stark pointed out. "You really want to find out what it's like when you can't see him coming? I've known Hank Pym for a long time; he's no security risk." Stark paused, considering S.H.I.E.L.D.'s options.

"Unless we make him one," he added, and now he sounded worried. Mitchell Carson glared at Stark, but for the moment he let it go.

CHAPTER 1

Scott Lang stood waiting for the punch to come. He was ready. It wouldn't be that bad.

But then the punch landed like a hammer hitting him in the right eye, and Scott reeled back into the line of other prisoners assembled to watch his fight with Peachy. "You like that?" Peachy taunted him. "You like that? Come get you some!"

Scott went after him. He charged into Peachy, who was a lot bigger than he was, and then stood up to throw a punch into Peachy's gut. Peachy looked fat, but when

Scott punched him it was like hitting a stone wall. "You didn't even move," Scott complained.

Peachy shrugged. "Nah."

"I mean, what if I come in on the left side, right...?" Scott stepped up to Peachy again and outlined what he was talking about, miming a half-speed punch. "Just out here, and see this one, and—"

As Peachy looked down, Scott hit him hard with a straight right. Peachy's head snapped around, but he didn't go down. Scott didn't know what he'd have to do to him to actually knock him down. The convicts roared, and Peachy, with a little smear of blood on his lip, looked up at Scott.

Uh-oh, Scott thought. *Might have gone too far there.*

Then a broad smile broke across Peachy's bearded face. "I'm gonna miss you, Scott."

Scott grinned back. "I'm gonna miss you, too, Peachy." They exchanged handshakes and hugs. "Man, you guys got the weirdest good-bye rituals."

"All right, break it up," the guards called, and an hour later Scott Lang was a free man.

He walked out past the prison gate, took his first breath of free air in a few years, and heard the unmistakable sound of his former cell mate Luis's voice. "Scotty! What's up, man?"

Luis was calling from across the visitor parking lot, his arms spread wide and a big grin on his face. "Hey, man," Scott called back, heading over to slap backs and get reacquainted.

"Hey, what's up with your eye?" Luis said, seeing the butterfly bandages on Scott's right eyebrow.

"Oh, well, what do you think? Peachy. His going-away present."

"Oh, yeah, I still got my scar from a year ago," Luis said, pointing to his own right eyebrow.

Scott could see the little ridge of scar tissue even though his eyebrow mostly covered it up. "Oh yeah."

"Yeah, yeah, yeah," Luis said. "You know what? I'm still the only one to knock him out."

"Well, I definitely didn't," Scott said as they got into

the ancient brown van Luis had driven all the way to the prison so he could meet Scott. It was a long drive from San Francisco, and Scott was looking forward to every minute of it. He'd served his time and now he was going to savor his freedom. Start a new life. Reconnect with his daughter.

"Thanks for picking me up, brother," he said a little while later as they drove down a mountain road toward the interstate.

"Oh, now, you think I'm gonna miss my cell mate getting out?"

You meet a lot of bad people in prison, Scott thought, *but you meet some good ones, too.* Luis was one of the good ones. "Hey, how's your girl, man?" he asked.

"Oh, she left me."

"Oh."

"Yeah, my mom died, too." Scott got quiet. A minute later, Luis added, "And my dad got deported." Now Scott really didn't know what to say, but a second later Luis brightened up. "But I got the van!"

Scott tried to get in the spirit. "It's nice."

"Yeah, right?"

"Thanks for the hookup, too," Scott added. "I needed a place to stay."

"You wait till you see this couch," Luis said, like he was describing a room at the Ritz. "You're gonna be really happy. You're gonna be on your feet in no time—watch."

"I hope so."

"Yeah. And I gotta introduce you to some people, some really skilled people."

"Not interested," Scott said immediately. He knew what Luis was talking about. Luis wanted Scott to get back into the life—the same life that had landed Scott in prison to begin with.

"Yeah, right!" Luis scoffed.

Every convict says he's going straight when he gets out of jail. Scott knew that, and he also knew that most cons didn't stick to the promise. But he was going to. "No, I'm serious, man. I'm not going back. I got a daughter to take care of."

Luis got serious, too, which was pretty unusual for him. "You know that jobs don't come easy for ex-cons, right?"

"Look, man, I got a master's in electrical engineering, all right?" Scott was looking forward to putting that degree to use. It had been a while since he'd gotten sidetracked into his life of crime. They were coming up to the bridge. San Franciso glittered in the distance. Scott felt good. "I'm gonna be fine," he said.

CHAPTER 2

Scott was remembering that conversation a week or so later, when, after applying for every job he could think of, he ended up working the counter at an ice cream shop. "Welcome!" he said, trying to sound cheerful. "Would you like to try our mango smoothie?"

"Uh, no thanks," the customer said. He looked at the menu, but Scott didn't think he'd actually read it, judging from what he said. "Um, I will have... I'll have a burger, please."

"Oh, we don't... we don't make that," Scott said.

"Pretzel. Hot pretzel, like, mustard...in mustard dip?"

Trying to be patient, Scott said, "It's ice cream."

"I'll just do with whatever's hot and fresh," the customer said.

Scott shook his head. "Dude," he said. *Some people...*

His manager, Dale, called from his office doorway. "Can I see you in the back, chief?" Scott looked over at him. "Pronto," Dale added.

"Sure thing, Dale," Scott said. He turned to his coworker, a teenage girl who treated Scott like he was somebody's grandfather. "Darby, could you just, uh... take care of this idiot? Thanks."

He walked back to his manager's office and found Dale sitting at his desk, arms folded. "Hey, Dale."

"Come on in. Pull up some chair." Dale picked up a folder from his desk. "Three years in prison, huh?"

Scott sighed. "You found out."

"We always find out," Dale said, as if they were some kind of super-secret spy agency instead of an ice cream chain.

"Look, I'm sorry, all right, but I...No one would hire me." Scott didn't know what else to say.

"Breaking and entering," Dale said. "Grand larceny."

"Look, I'm—I'm sorry, I, you know, it was..." Scott was floundering. "I—I don't do it anymore, I just try to..."

Then Dale caught him completely by surprise and threw Scott a salute. "Respect," he said. "I couldn't be happier about it."

Scott blinked. "Really?"

"Yeah, yeah." Over Scott's thanks, Dale went on, a goofy smile on his face like he was talking to a celebrity. "You really stuck it to those billionaires, and the more I read about what you did and stuff, I'm like...'Wow, I know this guy? I'm in charge of this guy? Wow!'"

Scott had never been congratulated for his criminal career before, and so he wasn't sure what to say. He decided to stay grateful. "Well, I'm very happy in this job, and I'm...I really just appreciate the opportunities and—"

"Yeah, yeah...Well, you're fired, of course." Dale still had that weird smile on his face. "I can't really keep you on."

For the second time in a few seconds, Scott blinked in surprise. "Wait, what? Fired?"

Dale nodded. "Yeah."

"Dale, look, it wasn't a violent crime," Scott protested. "I mean, I'm a good worker."

"No, it wasn't a violent crime. It was a cool crime." Now Scott was completely confused. Dale admired him and was firing him all at once. "I'll tell you what, though," Dale went on. "This'd be totally off the books, off the records, but, uh...if you want to grab you one of those mango smoothies on your way out the door, I'll just pretend I didn't see it."

Scott took it. Why not? It was all he was going to get.

He walked back to the hotel room he shared with Luis and found a huge party going on one floor down. The hotel was not a quiet place. Luis was stirring something at the kitchen counter. "Hey, Scotty, what's up?" he said. "I thought you were supposed to be at work."

"I was," Scott said glumly. "I got fired."

"They find out who you are?"

"Yeah."

Like everyone knew it, Luis said, "They always find out, bro."

Scott noticed two other guys sitting at the kitchen table, one tapping away at a laptop and the other just hanging out.

One moment of seriousness was about all Luis could manage. "You want some waffles?"

"Yeah, I'll take a waffle."

Luis noticed Scott eyeing the two newcomers. "Oh. That's Kurt. He was in Folsom for five years. He's a wizard on that laptop."

"Nice to meet you," Kurt said.

"Yeah, nice to meet you, too," Scott said. He had a bad feeling about why Luis would have a hacker in the room. "And who are you?" he asked the second guy.

"Dave." After a long pause, Dave added, "Nice work on the Vista job."

"Vista job? Yes," Kurt said. He had a thick Russian accent. "No, no, I have heard of this robbery."

Word gets around, Scott thought. "Well, technically, I

didn't rob them. Robbery involves threat. I hate violence; I burgled them. I'm a cat burglar."

"You mean you're a wuss," Dave said.

Scott thought about this. "Yeah."

Luis knew Kurt hadn't heard the whole Vista story, so he launched into it while he served the waffles. "They were overcharging the customers, right? And it added up to millions. He blows the whistle and he gets fired. And what does he do? He hacks into the security system and transfers millions back to the people that they stole it from. Posts all the bank records online."

"And he drove dude's Bentley into a swimming pool," Dave added, his voice full of admiration.

Scott pinned Luis with a look. "What are you doing? Hm?"

Luis played innocent. "Oh, I..."

"Why are you telling my life story to these guys? What do you want?"

Luis gave up pretending. "Okay," he said. "My cousin talked to this guy two weeks ago about this little, perfect job."

"No way," Scott said. He took another bite of waffle.

"No, no, no, wait! This guy, this guy fits your MO."

"No! I'm finished, man. I'm not going back to jail."

But Luis wasn't going to let it go. "It's some retired millionaire living off his golden parachute. It's a perfect Scott Lang mark."

"I don't care," Scott said. If this was how it was going to be living with Luis, he was going to look for another place to live. "I'm out."

CHAPTER 3

It had been a long time since Hank Pym paid a visit to the headquarters of the company that bore his name. The security guard at the gate did a double take when he pulled up. "Dr. Pym?"

"Yes. I'm still alive," Pym said, half-amused and half-irritated.

Inside, at the lobby checkpoint, he emptied his pockets into the tub for inspection and passed through the metal detector. "ID," the guard said.

Pym nodded past the guard. "Perhaps that will suffice."

Following Pym's look, the guard noticed the huge oil portrait of a younger Hank Pym, hung prominently on the wall. "Very sorry, sir," he said immediately. "Please come in."

"Is that Hank Pym?" a younger worker said as Hank strolled through the inside lobby. Hank didn't say anything. He was nervous about the day for a lot of reasons, and he wasn't good at small talk even in the most relaxed circumstances.

A familiar voice caused him to turn. "Good morning, Hank."

"Hope," he said, greeting his daughter and again feeling the ache of guilt and regret that came from their estrangement. "Would it kill you to call me Dad?"

She ignored the question. "Well, Dr. Cross will be so pleased that you could find time to join us today."

"More like thrilled," said a grinning Darren Cross, approaching Hank with his hand stuck out.

"And I'm surprised to receive any kind of invitation from you, Darren," Hank said, shaking Cross's hand. There was bad blood between them having to do with Cross's desire to run the company himself and take it in a direction Hank didn't approve. "What's the occasion?"

"Oh, you'll see," Cross said. "Won't he, Hope?"

All she said was "We're ready for you inside." Then she turned and headed toward a locked door that led to an adjacent presentation room.

"Ouch!" Cross said, trying to commiserate but not quite coming across as genuine. "I guess some old wounds never heal, huh?" He guided Hank toward the door, where Hope waited. "Don't worry. She's in good hands. You're in for a treat."

Pym didn't trust Cross, and he trusted him even less when he saw that one of the other attendees at this event was Mitchell Carson. "Long time no see, Dr. Pym," Carson said, barely disguising his hostility. "How's retirement?"

"How's your face?" Pym answered. He wanted to take another swing at Carson, but this was 2015, not 1989.

Carson didn't say anything, but the look he gave Pym was full of hate. Hope opened the door. "After you," she said.

One of these days he and Carson would have to really settle things between them, Pym thought. But that day hadn't quite arrived. Hope was a different and touchier issue. He still wanted to one day have a real relationship again, but he didn't know how to begin.

Darren Cross led the small group of contractors and politicians into a lab space populated by white-coated techs and full of sophisticated machinery. Pym had designed much of it himself before retiring. He took pride in seeing it still in use after so many years. Cross went down a short staircase to the main lab floor and stood in the center of the room.

"Now, before we start, I'd like to introduce a very special guest," he said. "This company's founder and my mentor, Dr. Hank Pym." Hank stood quietly as the techs and onlookers applauded him. He enjoyed the respect, but Cross's tone also kind of made him feel like a relic of another time.

Then he saw that Cross was standing next to a tabletop resin model of the building in which all of them stood— only the Pym logo on the wall was replaced by the legend

CROSS INDUSTRIES. Cross saw him notice, and he gave Pym a little smile. Now Hank wanted to punch him, too. Did he think he could just erase the name *Pym* from this company? If that was Cross's plan, Hank Pym wasn't going to make it easy. But first he would have to hear Cross out and understand what the plan really was.

"When I took over this company for Dr. Pym," Cross went on, "I immediately started researching a particle that could change the distance between atoms while increasing density and strength. Why this revolutionary idea remained buried beneath the dust and cobwebs of Hank's research, I couldn't tell you. But just imagine. A soldier the size of an insect."

He touched a remote control and three large video screens on the wall lit up. They played old footage of a battle between armed men and an invisible adversary who knocked them sprawling and threw them around the battlefield like they were toys. "The ultimate secret weapon," Cross said.

Occasionally the footage paused and zeroed in on a tiny flying figure. You couldn't see it when the footage moved at normal speed or when everything was in a regular perspective—but someone had done a lot of work to find the minuscule fighter in these old films and call attention to him. Hank got an uneasy feeling in the pit of his stomach.

"An 'Ant-Man,'" Cross said, and chuckled at how silly his own phrase sounded. "That's what they called you. Right, Hank?"

A murmur spread through the room as everyone present started to understand what Cross was really saying. Hank couldn't bring himself to look at Mitchell Carson, who must have been in on the whole thing. Cross was forcing this out into the open, and Hank was caught unprepared. Now Hank knew why Cross had wanted him here, but it was too late to do anything about it.

Cross froze the video again, this time on a frame that showed the tiny figure in a silver-and-red suit, punching through a pane of glass and leaving a hole that looked like it might have been made by a BB gun. "Silly, I know. Propaganda. Tales to astonish!" He climbed the stairs and stood next to Hank before going on. "Hank, will you tell our guests what you told me every single time I asked you, 'Was the Ant-Man real?'"

"Just a tall tale," Hank said, playing to the crowd a little because he still wasn't sure where Cross was going with this. He couldn't be planning to take it public, but there were a lot of S.H.I.E.L.D. officials and defense-industry bigwigs in the room. Hank had a bad feeling.

"Right," Cross said. He turned back to the room. "Because how could anything so miraculous possibly be real?"

The lab door opened and Cross led the group out. He didn't say another word until they were in a smaller, darker chamber, circular in shape, its walls lined with screens playing loops of different objects being miniaturized. "Well, I was inspired by the legend of the Ant-Man," he said. "And with my breakthrough, shrinking inorganic material, I thought, could it be possible to shrink a person? Could that be done? Well, it's not a legend anymore."

He touched a switch, and what looked like a large lens in a steel housing descended from the ceiling. A moment later, as Cross flicked through different resolutions, Hank figured out that the lens was actually a magnifying glass. Inside the housing, something came into view. A tiny yellow-and-black armored suit on a pedestal.

"Distinguished guests, I am proud to present the end of warfare as we know it: the Yellowjacket."

No, Hank thought. This was exactly what he had always feared. This was why he had kept the Pym Particle technology away from S.H.I.E.L.D. back in the '80s.

Now Cross had found it. "The Yellowjacket is an all-purpose weapon of war," he announced. "Capable of altering the size of the wearer for the ultimate combat advantage."

Cross started a promo video featuring a deep voiceover that struck Hank as more than a little menacing. "We live in an era in which the weapons we use to protect ourselves are undermined by constant surveillance." Fragmented camera views spilled across the screens. "It's time to return to a simpler age, when the powers of freedom can once again operate openly to protect their interests." Now the screens showed the Yellowjacket suit in action, with caption windows outlining its capabilities. Weapons systems, advanced sensors...and of course the ability to change its size to avoid detection. "An all-purpose peacekeeping vessel, the Yellowjacket can manage any conflict on the geopolitical landscape, completely unseen. Efficient in both preventative measures and tactical assault, practical applications include surveillance, industrial sabotage, and the elimination of obstructions on the road to peace."

The Yellowjacket in the video crawled through keyholes, hacked encrypted systems...and invisibly attacked unsuspecting human targets. "A single Yellowjacket offers the user unlimited influence to carry out protective actions," the voiceover went on. Then Hank got a deep chill as the video demonstrated what an army of Yellowjackets would look like deployed against human soldiers. "And one day soon, an army of Yellowjackets will create a sustainable environment of well-being around the world." As the voiceover ended, the Yellowjackets dissolved into an army of yellow dots spreading over a map of the earth—which then transformed into a Cross Technologies logo.

Hank looked over at Hope. From the expression on her face, he didn't think she had known this was coming.

The assembled S.H.I.E.L.D. and defense contractors took a moment to consider what they had just seen. The first person to speak sounded skeptical. "So it's a suit," he said.

"Don't be crude, Frank," Cross said, sounding both

amused and offended. "It's not a suit, it's a…it's a vessel. What's the matter, you're not impressed?"

"Oh, I'm impressed," Frank said. "I'm also concerned. Imagine what our enemies could do with this tech."

"We should have a longer conversation about that, Frank. I really value your opinion," Cross said in a tone that made it clear he meant the opposite. Then he turned to the rest of the room. "Thank you for coming. Hope?"

"Thank you very much, everybody," Hope said. She indicated the way back to the lobby. "I will escort you out now. Thank you."

As the rest of the group left, Cross and Hank were left alone. "You seem a bit shocked," Cross said.

"Darren, there's a reason I buried these secrets," Hank said quietly. Having the Ant-Man technology in wide use…Who could tell what rogue states or groups could do with it? Hank hadn't even trusted S.H.I.E.L.D. to do the right thing.

"So you finally admit it," Darren said with real emotion in his voice. Hank remembered when Darren was younger, full of optimism and thirst for knowledge. He'd looked up to Hank…and Hank had disappointed him.

27

Just like he had Hope. "We could have done this together, Hank," Cross went on. "But you ruined it." Then Cross took a moment to recover his composure. Cocky and self-assured again, he finished his little speech. "That's why you're the past and I'm the future."

"Don't do this," was all Hank could say.

"Dr. Cross," Mitchell Carson said. He had hung back when the rest of the group left, but Hank hadn't noticed until just then. "You sell to me first, twenty percent of your asking price, I can have the cash here in two weeks."

"Deal," Cross said immediately.

No, Hank thought. Not Mitchell Carson of all the people in the world. He had the ethics of a shark.

Cross and Carson left, and Hope was now the only other person in the room with Hank. When she was sure they were alone, she spoke quietly and urgently. "We have to make our move, Hank."

"How close is he?" Hank asked.

"He still can't shrink a live subject." She looked at him, his daughter whom he loved but didn't understand. "Just give me the suit," she said, almost begging. "Let me finish this once and for all."

"No," Hank said. He couldn't risk it. Couldn't risk her.

"I have Cross's complete trust," she said.

Hank knew what she meant. She could cut Cross Technologies apart from the inside and prevent Cross from selling the Yellowjacket tech to anyone, let alone Mitchell Carson. But she was still his daughter. "It's too dangerous."

"We don't have a choice."

"Well, that's not entirely true," Hank said. Even though Cross had been trying to keep him at a distance from the company's research, Hank had always suspected he would need to take action someday. So he'd started planning on his own. Hope wanted the suit, and he understood why, but Hank couldn't bear the thought of putting his daughter's life on the line. "I think I found a guy."

Now Hope looked perplexed. Also angry. "Who?"

CHAPTER 4

One good thing about the timing of his release from prison was that Scott could make his daughter Cassie's birthday party. He debated calling his ex-wife, Maggie, ahead of time but figured it would cause trouble, so he waited until a little after lunchtime and then just walked in the front door of Maggie's house—well, technically her fiancé Paxton's house. It was madness, exactly the way a house full of kids celebrating a birthday should be. Balloons, loud music, screaming—and there she was, little

Cassie, running down the hall toward him, shouting, "Daddy!"

"Peanut!" He dropped to his knees to scoop her into a big hug. "Happy birthday! I'm so sorry I'm late; I didn't know what time your party started."

"It was on the invitation!" she said, like he was the world's biggest doofus.

Then the complications started as Paxton—a big, muscular cop with no patience for his fiancé's ex-husband—appeared and said, "He didn't get an invitation." He shot a look at Scott. "But he came anyway." Paxton tried to keep his tone chipper, but Scott could tell he wasn't welcome.

"Well, I'm not going to miss my little girl's birthday party," he said to both of them.

"I'm gonna go tell Mommy you're here!" Cassie said, and dashed off.

"Oh, you don't…" Scott gave up. She'd find out sooner or later.

Paxton came up close. Too close. If they were in prison, Paxton would have been starting a fight. Scott had to suppress those prison instincts, though. He was back in the real world. Would have been nice to take a swing at Paxton, though. "What are you doing here, Lang?" he said. "You haven't paid a dime in child support. You know, right now if I wanted to, I could arrest you."

"Good to see you too, Paxton." Scott didn't want to make a scene in front of his daughter. Also, Paxton was technically correct. The other thing was that, even though he still loved Maggie, Scott knew Paxton was a fundamentally decent guy—for a cop—and was looking out for Maggie and Cassie in his way.

Cassie charged back into the room. "Mommy's so happy you're here, she choked on her drink," she said, and cracked up.

"Hey, look what I have for you." Scott handed her a gift bag.

"Can I open it now?" Cassie asked—but she asked Paxton, not Scott. That stung.

"Of course, sweetheart," Paxton said. "It's your birthday."

From the bag Cassie took the ugliest stuffed rabbit in the history of planet Earth. She squeezed it accidentally and it rasped out, "You're my bestest friend!"

Taken aback, Paxton said, "What is that thing?"

Cassie had a different reaction. "He's so ugly! I love him! Can I go show my friends?"

Paxton nodded. "Yeah, of course, sweetheart. Go ahead."

"You're my bestest friend!" the rabbit said again as she zipped off into the kitchen.

"Look," Scott said quietly. "The child support is coming, all right? It's just hard finding a job when you have a record."

Still facing him down, Paxton said, "I'm sure you'll figure it out, but for now, I want you out of my house."

"No way, it's my daughter's birthday!"

"It's my house!" Paxton said, his voice rising a notch.

Scott matched him. "So what? It's my kid!"

"Relax!" Maggie called as she came into the room. She didn't look happy to see Scott. "You can't just show up here. You know that; come on."

"It's a birthday party."

He could tell she didn't care. "Yeah, I know, but you can't just show up."

"She's my daughter." Didn't that matter? Scott knew he'd made some mistakes, but, man, what about second chances?

"You don't know the first thing about being a father," Paxton said.

Scott took a deep breath. Then, not looking at Paxton, he said, "Maggie, I tell you this as a friend and as the first love of my life: Your fiancé is a butthead."

"He's not a butthead," she objected.

Paxton chimed in. "Hey, watch your language."

"Oh, what language? I said 'head.'"

Scott would never have figured Maggie to get together with a prudish cop. But then again, Paxton was about as different from him as a man could be, so maybe that explained it.

She half guided, half pushed Scott out the door and shut it behind them.

"Really, Maggie? That guy?" Scott said when Paxton and Cassie were out of earshot. "Come on, you could marry anyone you want—you have to get engaged to a cop?"

"At least he's not a crook," she said evenly.

"I'm trying, okay? I've changed, uh..." She just looked at him, not buying it. Scott needed her to believe him. All he could tell her was the truth, knowing that every ex-con said the same things and he hadn't exactly given her any reason to trust him over the past few years. "I'm straight, I had a job, and...I want to provide. I've had a lot of time to think about it, and I love her. So much. I've missed so much time and I want to be a part of her life. What do I do?"

After a pause, Maggie said, "Get an apartment. Get a job, pay child support. And then we will talk about visitation, I promise." Something unclenched in Scott's chest. There was a chance. "You're her hero, Scott," Maggie added. "Just be the person she already thinks you are."

Right, he thought. *I can do that. I will do that.*

Cassie, with Paxton right behind her, came out to wave good-bye as Scott got in Luis's van and headed off, honking the van's goofy musical horn and shooting Cassie a wink. She laughed. Paxton did not.

Darren Cross thought the presentation had gone almost perfectly. He'd already made a deal for the Yellowjacket— for a lot of money. Mitchell Carson wanted the system badly. Also, Cross had shown Hank Pym that he was the future of the business. Pym's secret was out, at least within the company, and Cross was in control. The only hiccup was Frank's reluctance to get on board. Cross liked Frank, and valued him as an engineering consultant, but they needed to have a conversation.

So he walked into the executive washroom after the meeting had broken up and caught Frank washing his hands. "I'm sorry you have such deep concerns about the Yellowjacket, Frank."

"Yeah, well, uh, unfortunately we can't just do whatever we want," Frank said. "Would be nice though, right? But there are laws."

"What laws? Of man?" Cross realized that Frank really didn't understand what the Yellowjacket project meant. So he explained it a little. "The laws of nature transcend the laws of man. And I've transcended the laws of nature." He realized he was standing between Frank and the trash can, so Cross reached out and took the paper towel Frank had used to dry his hands.

"Darren, I don't think you understand," Frank said, but Cross had heard enough.

He'd designed a handheld version of the miniaturization technology and thought this might be the one that finally worked on a human subject. God knew he'd shrunk just about everything else with it already. Cross touched a button and a small electrical arc snapped out to touch Frank's chest.

Frank disappeared…and, looking down at the floor, Darren Cross realized the miniaturizer wasn't quite fully functional yet. "We still haven't worked out all the bugs," he apologized, and bent down with the paper towel to clean up the mess. "Good-bye, Frank."

You couldn't run a company like Cross Technologies without having everyone on board, he thought. That was just the way things were.

He had a dinner engagement with Hope that night, and thought he would use it to make sure she was completely on board, too.

CHAPTER 5

"You know," Darren said after he and Hope had been seated and served a glass of wine, "I've been thinking a lot about gratitude lately. Today, during my morning meditation, an interesting thought occurred to me and I think it might apply to you, too."

She looked at him, those snapping dark eyes under the curtain of her black bangs, and Cross fell a little bit more in love with her. "How's that?"

"Gratitude can be forgiveness," he said, and meant it. "I spent years carrying around my anger for Hank Pym.

I devoted my genius to him." Maybe that sounded arrogant, he thought, but it was true. Darren Cross knew how brilliant he was, and why should he pretend otherwise to Hope? "I could've worked anywhere. I chose my mentor poorly."

She listened. That was one of the things he really liked about Hope. She was an excellent listener. That was a rare thing. Everyone always wanted to talk. "You didn't even have a choice," Darren said. "He never believed in you. It's a shame what we had to do, but he forced us to do it, didn't he? But we shouldn't be angry; we should be grateful. Because his failures as a mentor, as a father, forced us to spread our wings."

He was being utterly sincere, but at the same time he was testing Hope a little. If she was angry or feeling guilty about the way Darren had manipulated her father's work—while keeping it secret from him—Darren had to know. He knew she'd talked to him after the presentation that morning, and although he would never ask her, Darren was burning to know what they'd said.

But most important, he had to know she was on his side.

"You're a success, Darren," Hope said with a dazzling

smile that stole his heart once and for all. "You deserve everything coming your way."

She understood, Darren thought. Good. They would move forward together. Hank Pym's faults and failures didn't have to doom them, too.

Scott tried every way he could think of to make the math work. If he took the income from a minimum-wage job, subtracted rent, child support, and all the other debts still hanging over his head from his time in prison... according to what Maggie had said that afternoon, in a little over a year she would let him start having visitation with Cassie.

More than a year.

No, he thought. *I can't handle that. I've already missed too much.*

But what else could he do?

When he got back to the hotel room, Luis and David were playing a video game. Kurt was of course glued to his laptop. "Stop cheating," David grumbled as Scott headed for the fridge.

Luis heard Scott come in, and called out, "Hey, what's up, hotshot?"

"Maybe he didn't hear you," David suggested when Scott didn't answer.

"How was the party?" Luis said, a little louder.

Scott had found a drink in the fridge. He popped it open, took a long swig, and said, "Tell me about that tip."

"Wha?" Luis dropped the game controller and stood up.

"I wanna know about that tip," Scott repeated.

"Oh, baby, it's on!" Luis shouted.

"Hot dog!" Kurt added. The expression sounded weird in his thick accent.

Luis looked like he might be about to explode from the excitement. "It's so on right now!"

"Calm down, all right?" Scott was all business. This was one of the most important decisions of his life and he needed to know every detail about it before he took the final step. "I just need to know where it came from. It's gotta be airtight."

"Okay," Luis said. He took a deep breath, and Scott knew he wasn't going to get the short version of the story. "I was at a party with my cousin Ernesto. And he tells me about this girl Emily we used to kick it with. She's working as a housekeeper now, right? And she's dating this dude Carlos from across the bay and she tells him about the dude that she's cleaning for. Right? That he's, like, this big-shot CEO that is all retired now, but he's loaded. And so Carlos and Ernesto are on the same softball team and they get to talking, right? And here comes the good part."

About time, Scott thought. He'd already lost track of who was saying what to whom, or what he was supposed to be getting from the bit about the softball team.

Luis caught his breath and went on, acting out the different parts as he told the rest of the story. "Carlos says, 'Yo, man. This guy's got a big safe just sitting in the basement. Just chillin'.' Of course Ernesto comes to me 'cause he knows I've got mad thieving skills. Of course I ask him, 'Did Emily tell Carlos to tell you to get to me what kind of safe it was?' And he says, 'Naw, dog. All she said is that it's, like, super legit, and whatever's in it has gotta be good!'"

Luis beamed at the end of the story. Scott, completely lost, just said, "What?"

"Old man have safe," Kurt said helpfully.

"And he's gone for a week," Luis said.

"All right," Scott said. One of the keys to a good operation was knowing which details to keep and which to throw away, Scott thought. But with Luis, you always got everything all in a big avalanche and had to pick through it first to figure out what was important. "There's an old man, he's got a safe, and he's gone for a week. Let's just work with that."

CHAPTER 6

Once Scott had all the details, putting the job together wasn't that hard. Scott was among the best in the world at removing things from houses without their owners knowing. Luis and Kurt and David were also good. As a team, they thought of themselves as the Avengers of burglars. So they figured out a plan, got their roles sorted out, and within a couple of days they were good to go. David was driving, Luis was handling communications, and Scott would be going into the millionaire's house after the safe.

Kurt, as usual, was glued to his laptop, checking on the

team's preparations. "Landlines cut, cell signals jammed. No one will be making for distress call tonight," he said.

"All check," Scott said into the earbuds they were all using. Luis, Kurt, and David answered. They were all looped in.

"If the job goes bad, you know I got your back, right?" Luis said to Scott once the van was in position on the street outside the millionaire's house. It was on a street of fancy houses on the hill near San Francisco's famous Coit Tower.

"Don't worry, it's not gonna happen," Scott said. He hopped out of the van and moved quickly toward the house.

"I love it when he gets cocky," Luis said.

Scott vaulted the wall and climbed the outside of the house to a second-floor balcony. He attached an alarm bypass to the house's power panel. "Alarm is dead," Scott whispered through the comm channel. Ten seconds later he was inside. "All right, I'm moving through the house." He found a set of keys on a table inside the front door and took them downstairs. The safe was supposed to be in the basement.

The keys got him through the first door, but inside was another. And this one didn't just have a mechanical lock. "There's a fingerprint lock on the door."

"He's got a what?" Luis said. "Ernesto didn't tell me nothing about that. Aw, man, are we done?"

"Not necessarily," Scott said.

People left fingerprints all over their houses. Often you could lift one if you had the right stuff. A piece of clear tape to get it off a good surface, like a doorknob; then some glue to pour over the lifted print; then a little heat to make the glue set and keep the print firm for pressing against the scanner. After five minutes in the house's kitchen, Scott had a rubbery circle of glue with a perfect print in the middle of it. He skipped back down the stairs and took a deep breath before pressing the print on the scanner.

It beeped and the light on the panel turned green. Scott opened the door. "I'm in."

"No alarms have been triggered," Kurt said. He was monitoring every electronic item in the house, courtesy of some custom surveillance gear he had built on Luis's kitchen table. "He's in like the Flynn."

"Oh, man," Scott said when he saw the safe.

"What is it?" Luis sounded nervous.

"Well, they weren't kidding. This safe is serious."

"How serious we talkin', Scotty?"

"It's a Carbondale. It's from 1910. Made from the same steel as the *Titanic*."

"Wow," Luis said. "Can you crack it?"

"Well, here's the thing. It doesn't do so well in the cold. Remember what that iceberg did?"

"Yeah, man," Luis said. "It killed DiCaprio." He was referring to the movie, not actual history, but Scott let it go.

"Killed everybody," David added.

"Man, not kill the old lady," Kurt pointed out. "She still throw the jewel into the oceans."

Improvising again, Scott dug around in his bag. Safecrackers never went anywhere without a drill and a bottle of liquid nitrogen. Those two things could get you into 99 percent of the safes ever made. He drilled a small hole into the housing of the safe's main tumbler. Then he found a gallon jug of water and a funnel elsewhere in the basement. He poured the water in and then sprayed a good helping of liquid nitrogen in after it. Hiding around the corner behind an air mattress he had found on a nearby shelf, he waited, peeking at the safe every once in a while. Ice was forming on the outside of its door.

"What're you doing?" Luis asked.

"I poured water in the locking mechanism and froze it with nitrogen," Scott explained. "Ice expands, metal doesn't."

A minute later, Luis asked, "What are you doing now?"

"Waiting." Groaning noises came from inside the safe. "Waiting..."

A bolt popped out of the safe and shot across the basement into the air mattress. In the next few seconds, ten or twelve others followed...and then the safe door tipped forward and crashed to the floor. "Nice," Scott said. Just like he'd planned it. He might not be very good at real life, but he was very good at cracking safes.

He hopped over the fallen door and into the safe, which was the size of a walk-in closet. It was lined with shelves and a small table stood against its back wall. "What is it? Cash? Jewels?"

"There's nothing here," Scott said. Other than a couple

of jars on the shelves and a strange-looking leather suit and helmet on the table...*Who would want any of this stuff?* he wondered.

"What'd you say?" Luis sounded incredulous.

"It's a suit."

"What?"

Scott picked up the helmet. It had little antennae on it but otherwise looked just like a custom motorcycle helmet. The suit was silver and red and covered in dust. "It's an old motorcycle suit," he said, disgusted.

"There's no cash, no jewelry, nothing?"

"No." He slammed the helmet back down. "It's a bust."

"I'm really sorry, Scotty," Luis said. "I know you needed a score."

What the heck, he thought. He took the suit and helmet, just so he hadn't come for nothing.

CHAPTER 7

Back at the hotel, in the bathroom, after he'd washed his face and gotten over his disappointment, Scott looked at the suit and helmet. There was a belt and some other weird gear with it, and little vials of red fluid in the belt. "Why would you lock this up?" he wondered out loud. "So weird."

He decided to try them on. Why not? They must be valuable or they wouldn't have been in the safe. That was a rule of human nature. Nobody put things in safes unless they were valuable.

Once he got the suit and helmet on, he looked around. Things didn't seem much different. The helmet's visor kind of restricted his peripheral vision, but other than that it was just like wearing a fancy cycling suit—with a weird belt and gloves that had red buttons on them, at the base of each index finger. Right where it would be easy to push them with your thumb.

He heard the front door slam, and Luis called, "Scotty, what's up, man?"

Scott didn't want Luis to see him in the suit. He jumped into the bathtub and pulled the shower curtain closed. "I wonder..." he said to himself, looking at the buttons. "What is this?"

He pressed one. Nothing happened.

He pressed the other one. A lot happened.

Suddenly Scott was falling through space, a giant open space with a vast white floor below. After falling for a long time he hit the floor hard. When he got to his feet he looked around, wondering where he was...and then he figured it out.

He was still in the bathtub. Only the shower-drain plug

was the size of a boxing ring. The washcloth lying on the other side of the tub was the size of a basketball court.

No, that was wrong. They weren't bigger.

He was smaller.

"The world sure seems different from down here, doesn't it, Scott?" a voice said in his ear.

"What? Who... who said that?" Far above him, Scott saw Luis come into the bathroom and pull the shower curtain aside. "Luis!" he shouted. "Luis, I'm here!"

Luis didn't hear him. He bent toward the faucet. "It's a trial by fire, Scott," the voice in the helmet said. "Or in this case, water."

The water from the faucet was a flash flood, sweeping Scott up and flinging him straight to the other side of the tub. He rode the crest of the water up and into the air, then tumbled over the edge of the tub and smacked down onto the tile floor—which cracked at the impact. "Guess you're tougher than you thought," the voice commented.

Scott had other things on his mind. Namely, Luis undressing. "Oh, I don't want to see this," he said, and dodged Luis's clothes as they fell to the floor. But he wasn't looking where he was going, and he fell through a crack in the floor...then punched straight through the next floor, which slowed him down enough that when he landed on the turntable in the party room downstairs, he didn't even break the record. He spun around, screaming. The grooves in the vinyl record were big enough for him to hold on to—no, he was small enough to hold on to them. But the needle hit him and knocked him to the floor. The bass from the music practically bounced him around, and Scott ran through the party, dodging feet the size of battleships.

He screamed again as one of them stepped on him — but he wasn't hurt! Amazed, he kept running. He tripped on the edge of a heating grate and fell down through the duct. When he came out, he landed on a rug just in time to be vacuumed up with a bunch of dust. The vacuum shot him up into its bag so fast that he punched through the top of it. He ran through a crack in the wall, thinking maybe he'd be safe for a minute...

And there was a mouse the size of a brontosaurus. It chittered at him and lunged. Scott ran and jumped ahead of it onto a loaded mousetrap. His weight sprang the trap and he was catapulted through the hotel wall and out over the street. He landed on a car below and, even though he was still the size of a BB, the impact of his body left a dimple in the roof.

A moment later, he felt a surge and all of a sudden the world shrank back into place. No, he grew back to his regular size. Panting and terrified, he lay there spread-eagled on the roof of the car, trying to figure out what had just happened to him.

"Not bad for a test-drive," the voice in the helmet said. Scott slapped at it and the mask popped up. Rain fell on his face. "Keep the suit. I'll be in touch."

"No, no," he panted. "No. No, thank you." Nothing in the world would convince him to keep the suit if it meant he might go through that again.

Scott did the only thing he could think of: He broke into the house again and put the suit back that same night. Then, when he vaulted back over the wall and landed on the street, ready to go home, lights flashed everywhere and Scott was immediately surrounded by police. "You are under arrest!" one of them shouted, gun drawn.

"No, I didn't steal anything!" Scott said. "I was returning something I stole."

Oops, he thought. That was the wrong thing to say.

Sitting in jail later, Scott looked up to see Paxton on the other side of the bars. "You know you almost had us convinced you were going to change your ways? They were really rooting for you. This is going to break their hearts." He looked at Scott and Scott wished he could disappear.

Well, no. He'd just done that and it was terrifying.

Another cop came up to the bars. "You have a visitor."

"Who?"

"Your lawyer."

"My lawyer?" Scott hadn't called a lawyer.

The cop led him into a room where an older guy with a neat goatee and wearing a five-thousand-dollar suit sat at the table. "I told you I'd be in touch, Scotty," he said, and Scott recognized the voice. This was the guy who had talked to him inside the helmet. "I'm starting to think that you prefer the inside of a jail cell. Sit down."

Scott did. "Sir," he said, "I'm sorry I stole the suit. I don't even want to know why you have it."

"Maggie was right about you," the man said. Scott shut up. How did he know about Maggie? "The way she's trying to keep you away from Cassie..." he went on. "The moment things get hard, you turn right back to crime. The way I see it you have a choice. You can either spend the rest of your life in prison or go back to your cell and await further instructions."

"I don't understand," Scott said. He'd never said anything truer.

"I don't expect you to," the suit's owner said. "But you don't have many options right now. Quite frankly, neither do I. Why do you think I let you steal that suit in the first place?"

"What?" He'd been set up? How? And more important, why? All of a sudden Scott was wishing he was back at the ice cream shop.

"Second chances don't come around all that much. So next time you think you might see one, I suggest you take a real close look at it." The suit's owner got up and left. Scott didn't see the ants clearing away from the lens of the surveillance camera.

CHAPTER 8

Y ou are my bestest friend!" the weird rabbit said over and over again as Cassie snuggled down with it into bed.

Maggie sat on the side of her bed and finished tucking Cassie in. "Are you sure you don't want a different toy?"

"No," she said firmly. "I love this one."

"Okay." She didn't have much else from her father, Maggie thought. No wonder she clings to this. "Well, get some sleep, then. I love you."

"Mommy," Cassie said before Maggie got up from the bed.

"Hm?"

"Is Daddy a bad man? I heard some grown-ups say he's bad."

How did you explain Scott Lang to a little girl, Maggie wondered. He was complicated. Too complicated to stay married to, good-hearted but prone to doing dumb things. But bad? "No," Maggie said gently. "Daddy just gets confused sometimes, you know?"

Scott was sitting in his cell and wondering how much of the rest of his life he would spend counting cinder blocks and seeing patterns in chipped paint. He'd really made a mess of this job, and it was killing him that he'd gone and tried to take the stupid suit back. Why not just throw it out? Go downtown somewhere, find a Dumpster when nobody was looking, forget about the whole thing. But no—he'd gotten scared and wanted that thing away from him.

Truth was he'd also been scared that anyone who had a suit like that might be able to find him. Either way, trying to give it back had turned out to be the dumbest thing he'd ever done.

He looked down at the floor for a change of scenery from the wall and saw something moving. *Great*, he thought. *Jailhouse roaches*.

But they weren't roaches. They were ants.

Carrying a tiny, tiny version of the suit.

No way, Scott thought—and with a *whoosh* the suit expanded to full-size.

The old man had come through.

Now the ants were forming numbers on the floor. *10 . . . 9 . . . 8 . . .*

A message. A countdown. *Now or never*, Scott thought—and he got the suit on just as the cop who had processed him came down the hall. Scott hit the button and *bam*—he was a one-quarter inch tall and running as fast as he could under the bars, past the cop, and toward the door.

"Smart choice," the old man said in his ear. "You actually listened for once. Under the door."

Behind him, Scott heard the cops shouting at each other to set up a perimeter and start the search. He heard Paxton's voice among them. Scott ran under the door and out into the parking lot. It was full of police cars. "Okay. Where to now?"

"Hang tight," the old man said.

Ants appeared all around Scott, ringing him in and getting closer. He started shouting at them. "Get back, get back, get back!"

"Scott," the old man said. "These are my associates."

The lead ant had a camera attached to its thorax. "Huh? You got a camera on an ant?" Then Scott realized he was saying this while inside a suit that could change size. "Yeah, sure, why not? Where's the car?"

"No car. We've got wings," the old man said. "Incoming."

A huge flying ant swooped over Scott's head and landed next to him on the pavement. The beat of its wings sounded like a helicopter's rotors. "Put your foot on the central node and not the thorax," the old man said.

"Are you kidding? How safe is—"

"Get on the ant, Scott."

He did, and a few seconds later found himself hitching

a ride on the back of a flying ant...that was hitching a ride on a police car that roared down the street with lights and sirens at full blast.

"Why am I on a police car?" Scott shouted. "Shouldn't I not be on a police car?"

"So they can give you a lift past their five-block perimeter," the old man said.

That made sense, or at least as much sense as anything else right now. "All right. Now, what's the next move?"

"Hang on tight."

The ant crawled across the cop car's roof toward the rack holding its lights. "Oh, this is easy," Scott said. "I'm getting the hang of this. Yank up to go up. It's like a horse."

"You're throwing 247 off balance," the old man warned as the ant tipped to one side.

"Wait, his name is 247?"

"He doesn't have a name. He has a number, Scott. Do you have any idea how many ants there are?"

"Whoa!" Scott cried out as the ant took off from the car in a sudden rush of wind, landing on one of the car's side mirrors. Also upside down.

"Maybe it's 248?" the old man wondered.

Scott was completely disoriented by seeing the world going backward and upside down. "No, no, no, no, no! Vertigo, vertigo!"

"No, I think it's 247. Hang on," the old man said. The ant took off from the car and skillfully rode the airstream from a passing motorcycle.

Scott kept pulling on the lines attached to the harness on its back. "I think I'm getting the hang of this," Scott said. The ant seemed to be going where he wanted it to.

"I'm controlling 247. He is not listening to you."

"What?" The ant buzzed into and through one of San Francisco's famous streetcars, getting briefly tangled in a woman's hair. She twitched and flicked it away. "Can I make one little request?"

"No."

"Stop, 247," Scott pleaded. "Time-out, time-out." 247 skittered across a newspaper and out the back of the streetcar. "Just wait. Whoa!" The updraft from a manhole cover lifted them abruptly. "What happens if I throw up in this helmet?"

"It's my helmet, Scott. Do not throw up."

"Just set 'er down, all right? I'm getting light-headed."

Ahead of them was the Coit Tower. They were flying to the old man's house, Scott thought. He didn't feel like he was going to throw up anymore, but something was... he was getting dizzy, having trouble hanging on to the ant.

"Hang on, Scott," the old man warned.

"Yeah, I'm getting a little light... it's funny..." Scott tried to say something else, but his head was spinning, and in the next moment he felt himself start to fall.

CHAPTER 9

The next thing Scott remembered was waking up to a striking dark-haired woman tapping on her phone in the corner of a bedroom. "Hello," he said uncertainly.

She ignored him. "Who are you?" he asked. "Have you been standing there watching me sleep this whole time?"

"Yes," she said.

"Why?"

"Because the last time you were here you stole something." She put her phone away and looked at him.

"Oh." Scott knew where he was now. In the old man's

house. The bed was nice, the room was nice, but he wanted to get out. He couldn't stay there. "Hey, look," he said, throwing back the covers and swinging his feet off the bed.

That's when he noticed the carpet around the bed was crawling with ants. Huge ones. "Whoa!" He pulled his feet back and stared down at them.

"*Paraponera clavata*," the woman said. "Giant tropical bullet ants ranked highest on the Schmidt pain index. They're here to keep an eye on you when I can't." She paused to let that sink in. "Dr. Pym's waiting for you downstairs."

"Who?" She left without saying anything else. "Hey," he called after her. "Um, whose pajamas are these?"

She didn't come back, and the carpet was still covered in bullet ants. Scott didn't know what the Schmidt pain index was, but if these ants rated highest on it, he was pretty sure he didn't want them to bite him. "How am I supposed to do this?"

She'd said Dr. Pym was waiting. Then she'd left. Therefore, Scott reasoned, she must want him to follow. So the ants would...

Gingerly he lowered one foot to the carpet. The ants crawled out of the way. Scott put his other foot down. Same deal. "Just one step at a time," he said. He walked slowly through the ants, talking to them on the way. "You don't bite me, I don't step on you—deal?"

He found the old man—Dr. Pym—sitting with coffee at his dining room table, reading the paper. The woman was there, too. "I could take down the servers and Cross wouldn't even know," she was arguing as Scott walked in. "We don't need this guy."

Pym saw Scott coming in. "I assume that you've already met my daughter, Hope," he said.

So that was her name, Scott thought. "I did." He paused, feeling like he should say something else. "She's great."

"She doesn't think that we need you," Pym said.

"We don't," she said. "We can do this ourselves."

Scott sat as Pym said irritably, "I go to all this effort to let you steal my suit, and then Hope has you arrested."

"Okay," she said. "We can try this and when he fails I'll do it myself."

Fails at what? Scott wondered. He hadn't had a chance to fail at anything yet, if you didn't count trying to return the suit. "She's a little bit anxious," Pym said. "It has to do with this job, which, judging by the fact that you're sitting opposite me, I take it you're interested in."

Whoa, Scott thought. *Not so fast.* "What job?"

Ignoring the question, Pym nodded at the cup in front of Scott on the table. "Would you like some tea?"

Oh. Not coffee. "Uh, sure," Scott said.

"I was very impressed with how you managed to get past my security system. Freezing that metal was particularly clever."

How far back did the setup go? Scott already knew the job wasn't on the up and up, but Pym was basically saying he'd maneuvered Scott through the whole process. "Were you watching me?"

"Scott, I've been watching you for a while, ever since you robbed Vista Corp. Oh, excuse me, *burgled* Vista Corp." He tapped one of the newspapers on the table. Scott saw his face under a headline about the Vista job. "Vista's security system is one of the most advanced in the business. It's supposed to be unbeatable but you beat it. Would you like some sugar?"

"Yeah, thanks." Ants started pushing sugar cubes

across the table and Scott changed his mind. "You know what, I'm okay." The ants turned around and pushed the cubes back the way they'd come. "How do you make them do that?"

"Ants can lift objects fifty times their weight. They build, farm, they cooperate with each other." Clearly this Dr. Pym had a thing for ants.

"Right. But how do you make them do that?" The ants were putting the sugar cubes back in the little cup. Scott figured this trick had a name, but he didn't know what it was.

Pym tapped a little earpiece Scott hadn't seen until just then. "I use electromagnetic waves to stimulate their olfactory nerve center. I speak to them. I can go anywhere, hear anything, and see everything."

"And still know absolutely nothing," Hope said. *Man,* Scott thought. *This is not a close father-daughter relationship.* "I'm late to meet Cross," she added, standing to leave.

Scott raised his hand. "Uh...Dr. Pym?"

"You don't need to raise your hand, Scott."

"Sorry, I just have one question. Who are you, who is she, what the heck's going on, and can I go back to jail now?" That was four questions, but the last one was the most important. Scott had been played like a fish up to this point, and he felt like he was in way over his head. He wanted out while he could still get out, and before someone got mad at him and sent a horde of telepathically controlled bullet ants after him or something. Jail had to be better than that.

Pym looked at Scott for a long moment without answering any of his questions. Then he simply said, "Come with me."

CHAPTER 10

Down in the basement, across from the safe Scott had cracked, Pym tapped a code into a hidden door. It opened with a series of beeps, exposing a large lab space. Scott couldn't help but wonder how he'd built it. They must have been out under the street. "Twenty years ago I created a formula that altered atomic relative distance," Pym said.

"Huh?" Scott had no idea what that meant.

"I learned how to change the distance between atoms. That's what powers the suit, that's why it works." Pym led

Scott into the lab, which was full of electronic gizmos that made Scott's engineer-trained fingers twitch.

"Wow," he said. He'd always wanted a lab like this. Then he saw there were ants everywhere in here, too.

"It was dangerous," Pym went on. "Too dangerous. So I hid it from the world. And that's when I switched gears and I started my own company."

"Pym Tech."

"Yes." Pym was digging around in a duffel bag he'd taken out of a locker. "I took on a young protégé called Darren Cross."

"Darren Cross." Scott knew the name. "He's a big deal."

Pym had vials of the red fluid in his hands. "But before he was a big deal he was my assistant. I thought I saw something in him, a son I never had, perhaps." He set up the vials on a work table next to a glass case full of ants crawling through tunnels they'd made in some kind of white substance. "He was brilliant, but as we became close he began to suspect that I wasn't telling him everything. He heard rumors about what were called the Pym Particles, and he became obsessed with re-creating my formula."

Pym held up one of the vials. Scott guessed they had Pym Particles in them. That's what gave the suit its shrinking ability. "But I wouldn't help him, so he conspired against me and he voted me out of my own company."

Scott didn't know much about how big corporations worked, but that sounded weird to him. "How could he do that?"

"The board's chairman is my daughter, Hope. She was the deciding vote." It hurt Pym to remember this; Scott could see that. He didn't stop, though. "But she came back to me when she saw how close Cross was to cracking my formula."

Scott took all this in as Pym set the suit's helmet on the table. "The process is highly volatile. What isn't protected by a specialized helmet can affect the brain's chemistry. I don't think Darren realizes this, and, you know, he's not the most stable guy to begin with."

This was all useful information, Scott thought. But it wasn't telling him what he really wanted to know. "So, what do you want from me?"

Pym looked up from his work. "Scott, I believe that everyone deserves a shot at redemption. Do you?"

"I do," Scott said. He meant it, too. He wanted that shot more than anything.

"If you can help me, I promise I can help you be with your daughter again." Scott believed he could. A guy with Pym's money and clout could be a big help with the court. "Now, are you ready to redeem yourself?"

"Absolutely," Scott said. Whatever he'd gotten himself into here, he knew one thing for certain. "My days of breaking into places and stealing stuff are done. What do you want me to do?"

Pym cracked a little smile. "I want you to break into a place and steal some stuff."

Maggie, Paxton, and Cassie were sitting at breakfast when Paxton's phone chimed. "You going to be home for dinner tonight?" Maggie asked him at the same time.

"Uh, yeah," he said, distracted by the phone. It was a text from his partner, Gale: *Lang's "LAWYER" is Dr. Hank Pym, as in Pym Tech.* Below it was a picture of Pym. *Whoa,* Paxton thought. *This puts a new spin on things.* "I'll pick something up, okay?" He got up, suddenly anxious to be back on the case.

"Okay." She nodded at the phone still in his hand. "Good news?"

"Uh, I don't know." How did a guy like Scott Lang get Hank Pym's attention? And why was Pym lying about being Lang's lawyer, especially when Lang had been caught coming out of Pym's house? "It's news."

"Are you trying to find my daddy?" Cassie asked.

"Yeah, I am, sweetheart." He wasn't sure what to say, so he went with a half-truth. "I just want your daddy to be safe."

"Hope you don't catch him." She dug back into her cereal. Maggie and Paxton exchanged a look. The situation, they knew, was going to get more difficult before it got easier—if it ever did.

In a lab deep inside the Pym Tech complex, Darren Cross hit the switch that would test the miniaturization beam on another experiment in a long line of living subjects. None of them had yet survived. Mice, sheep... the beam had killed them all. But Cross was not going to quit. Not ever. He was close, and when he had the miniaturization down, the Yellowjacket system wasn't just going to make him rich—it was going to make him one of the most powerful men on earth. Not even the Avengers had tech like this.

The yellow fluid in the feeder tubes compressed and the beam flashed out into a glass box holding a three-month-old lamb. Cross held his breath, waiting for the afterimage of the flash to leave his eyes.

He looked at the table and at first saw nothing. Then his eyes registered a tiny version of the glass box...and inside it, a tiny version of the lamb.

I did it, he thought. *At last, I did it.*

From an observation room next to the lab, Hope Pym watched.

CHAPTER 11

P ym sat Scott down at a big video screen and started explaining the importance of the job he wanted Scott to do. "This isn't the first time these guys have tried to get their hands on game-changing weaponry," he said, pointing out a particular person on the screen. "That's Mitchell Carson, ex–head of defense at S.H.I.E.L.D., presently in the business of toppling governments. He always wanted my tech. And now, unless we break in and steal the Yellowjacket and destroy all the data, Darren Cross is gonna unleash chaos upon the world." Scott gathered that Cross was planning to sell the Yellowjacket thing—which was a version of Pym's original suit, only with weapons—to this Carson guy. It didn't sound good.

But it was a problem with an obvious solution that maybe hadn't occurred to Pym. "I think our first move should be calling the Avengers," Scott said.

Pym stood up and paced the room. "I've spent half my life trying to keep this technology out of the hands of a Stark. I'm not going to hand deliver it to one now. This is not some cute technology like the Iron Man suit. This could change the texture of reality. Besides, they're probably too busy dropping cities out of the sky."

"Okay, then, why don't you just send the ants?"

"Scott, they are ants. Ants, they can do a lot of things, but they still need a leader. Somebody that can infiltrate a place that's designed to prevent infiltration."

"Hank, I'm a thief," Scott said. "All right, I'm a good thief. But this is insane." The last guy in the world Scott wanted to rely on to save the world was himself.

"He's right, Hank, and you know it," Hope said from the doorway. Neither of them had heard her come in. "You've seen the footage; you know what Cross is capable of. I was against using him when we had months; now we have days. I'm wearing the suit."

Pym shook his head. "Absolutely not."

"I know the facility inside and out. I know how Cross thinks. I know this mission better than anybody here."

That was all true, Scott thought. But this was turning into a father-daughter thing again, and he stayed out of it. "We need you close to Cross, otherwise this mission cannot work," Pym said.

"We don't have time to screw around," she argued. Meaning, screw around getting some random thief up to speed.

Frustrated, Pym started to raise his voice again. "Hope, please, this is a—"

"He is a criminal. I'm your daughter." She was getting hot, too.

"No!" Pym shouted. In the silence that followed, they glared at each other and Scott wished he was anywhere else. Even prison. Then Hope, the hurt and disappointment plain on her face, left the room.

"She's right, Hank," Scott said quietly. "I'm not your guy. Why don't you wear the suit?"

"You think I don't want to?" Pym answered. "I can't. I spent years wearing it. It took a toll on me. You're our only option." He paused, his anger all gone and replaced with sadness. "Before Hope lost her mother, she used to look at me like I was the greatest man in the world. And now she looks at me and it's just disappointment. It's too late for me. But not for you. This is your chance. The chance to earn that look in your daughter's eyes. To become the hero that she already thinks you are." That echo of what Maggie had said to him the day before stung Scott. "It's not about saving our world," Pym finished. "It's about saving theirs."

"That was a good speech," Scott said after a moment.

Pym didn't care about the compliment. He cared about making his point. "Scott," he said, "I need you to be the Ant-Man."

And so Scott's training began. An hour later he was wearing the suit while Pym prepped him and Hope stood by watching, angry but staying with her father because the threat from Darren Cross was bigger than their argument. Scott was at one end of a hallway, Hope and Pym at the other.

"In the right hands, the relationship between man and suit is symbiotic," Pym said. "The suit has power, the man harnesses that power. You need to be skillful, agile, and above all, you need to be fast. You should be able to shrink and grow on a dime so your size always suits your needs."

Pym shut the door between them. "Now dive through the keyhole, Scott. You charge big, you dive small, then you emerge big."

Scott tried it. He mistimed the change and hit the door. "Ow!" He tried it again. "Ow!" And again. "Ow!"

Hope looked at her father as Scott hit the other side of the door one more time. "Useless," she said.

But she took over part of his training, too, in another area of the basement they rigged up as a gym. "When you're small, energy is compressed, so when you have the force of a two-hundred-pound man behind a fist a hundredth of an inch wide, you're like a bullet. You punch too hard, you kill someone; too soft, it's a love tap. In other words, you have to know how to punch."

"I was in prison for three years," Scott said. "I know how to punch."

She held up a hand like a sparring glove. "Show me." Scott did. "Terrible," she commented.

Irritated, he said, "You want to show me how to punch?" He held up his hand like she had. "Show me."

Faster than he could follow, her right hand snapped out and her fist caught Scott flush on the corner of his mouth. He staggered backward and sank down to the floor, eyes wide. She hit like Peachy.

"That's how you punch," she said.

"She's been looking forward to this," Pym said with a grin from nearby, where he was tinkering with the Ant-Man rig.

"No kidding," Scott said. His head was clearing.

"Hope trained in martial arts at a, uh, difficult time," Pym said.

She gave him an acid smile. "Oh, by 'difficult time,' he means when my mother died."

"We lost her in a plane crash," Pym explained to Scott.

"It's bad enough you won't tell me how she died," Hope said. "Could you please stop telling me that lie? We're working here." She turned away from him and back to Scott. "All right, princess, let's get back to work."

Back on his feet and all the way upright, Scott held up his hand again. "Were you going for the hand?" he asked. She just smiled.

Another part of his training was fiddling with the electronics in the Ant-Man suit, and the next day he was resoldering some of the connections in the regulator. He'd started to figure out how it all worked. Pym walked in and Scott said, "You know, I think this regulator is holding me back."

"Do not screw with the regulator," Pym said immediately. "If that regulator is compromised you would go subatomic."

"What does that mean?"

"It means that you would enter a quantum realm."

"What does that mean?"

"It means that you would enter a reality where all concepts of time and space become irrelevant as you shrink for all eternity." Pym spoke slowly, with deep emotion. This wasn't just a description to him. "Everything that you know, and love, gone forever."

Scott considered this. "Cool. Yeah. I'm…" He shrugged. "If it ain't broke…"

Pym had come in to show him the next training stage according to the plan he'd worked out with Hope.

"You've learned about the suit, but you've yet to learn about your greatest allies." He pointed at the wall lined with ant farms, each labeled with a different species name. "The ants. Loyal, brave, and your partners on this job." Pym had Scott suit up and head outside. While they sat on the porch, Scott shrank and entered an anthill in Pym's backyard. The first ant he got to know was *Paratrechina longicornis*. "Commonly known as crazy ants," Hope said over the suit's headset. "They're lightning fast and can conduct electricity, which makes them useful to fry out enemy electronics."

Scott saw one of them in the tunnel. Yellow and orange with a striped abdomen. It came right up to him, and when he knelt it climbed into his lap like a puppy. "Oh, you're not so crazy," he said, petting it. "You're cute."

A split second later he was covered in hundreds of them. "Aaah!" he screamed, exploding back to normal size and erupting up through Pym's lawn.

Hope and Pym stared at him.

"That was a lot scarier a second ago," he said, but he could tell they didn't believe him. They sent him right back down.

"Okay. Who's next?" he asked when he was back underground and shrank again.

"*Paraponera clavata.*"

Those he recognized. They loomed over him in the tunnel, twenty times the size of the crazy ants. "I know. Bullet ants, right? Number one on the Schmidt pain index." Scott decided he might as well talk to them. "Hey, guys! Remember me from the bedroom?"

When they came after him, he couldn't help it. He exploded through the lawn again.

Pym and Hope brought him inside for the next introduction. "*Camponotus pennsylvanicus,*" Pym said as Scott looked through a magnifying glass at the ant in question, which was crawling over an open book on the coffee table.

"Alternatively known as a carpenter ant. Ideal for ground and air transport."

"Wait a minute, I know this guy," Scott said. He was pretty sure it was the ant he'd ridden on the police car. 247. But now he needed a name. "I'm going to call him Ant-thony."

"That's good," Pym said. Scott couldn't tell if he was joking. "That's very good, because this time you're really going to have to learn how to control him." He set Scott up with some ants and some sugar cubes. "Tell them to put the sugar in the teacup."

Scott got to work.

CHAPTER 12

Hope kept up Scott's martial arts training, and he got better fast. She could still have kicked his butt if she'd wanted to, but at least he wasn't completely outclassed. Meanwhile he and Hope also analyzed the layout of the Pym Tech Futures Lab, where Darren Cross housed the Yellowjacket project.

"It looks like the lab has its own isolated power supply," Scott said, looking over a blueprint. That meant he wouldn't be able to cut the alarms from outside like he had with Pym's house.

"There's a security guard posted around the clock," she said. "We need you to take him out to deactivate the security systems."

Shouldn't be too hard, he thought, as long as the guard didn't see him coming.

Hope pulled up a schematic drawing of the case holding the prototype Yellowjacket suit. "The Yellowjacket pod is hermetically sealed and the only access point is a tube we estimate to be about five millimeters in diameter," she said.

Ah, Scott thought. *This is where it gets hairy.* "Why do I have a sick feeling in my stomach?"

Hope pulled up another view, this one showing the security on the pod itself. "The tube is protected by a laser grid and we can only power that down for fifteen seconds."

"You're going to need to signal the crazy ants to blow the servers, retrieve the suit, and exit the vaults before the backup power comes on," Pym said.

Scott nodded. It was possible. Not an easy job—a long way from it. But possible.

He was still thinking about that and dabbing some alcohol on the mat burns from his latest sparring session, when Hope stuck her head into the room and said, "Hank wants you outside for target practice."

When Scott got outside, Hank was holding two little discs, one in each hand. They looked like something a kid would shoot out of a toy gun. One was red and one blue. "The suit has no weapons, so I made you these discs," Hank said. "Red shrinks. Blue enlarges."

They practiced throwing them for a while, growing and shrinking various things out in Pym's yard, until Scott was reasonably sure he could hit something with them if he had to. Then it was back to meeting the various species of ants Pym kept, so Scott suited up and headed underground one more time. "*Solenopsis mandibularis.* Known for their bite, the fire ants have evolved into remarkable architects. They are handy to get you in and out of difficult places." While Pym said this, Scott ordered the fire ants to turn themselves into a bridge, and then ran across it. He had that down pretty good, but he was still having a hard time with the carpenter ants. They didn't want to put the sugar cubes in the teacup, even after days of effort.

"You can do it, Scott," Pym encouraged him. "Come on."

Scott stared at the ants on the table. They didn't do anything. *Come on, ants*, he thought. *Move the sugar cube!*

They still didn't do anything. He sat back and tossed the earpiece on the table in frustration. "They're not listening to me."

"You have to commit," Hope said. "You have to mean it. No shortcuts, no lies."

"Throwing insults into the mix will not do anyone any good, Hope," Pym commented.

"We don't have time for coddling," she pointed out. Cross was going to sell the Yellowjacket prototype any day now.

Pym knew this, which was why he wanted to avoid the conflicts with his daughter. "Our focus should be on helping Scott."

"Really? Is that where our focus should be?" Pym saw he'd wounded her. Scott saw it, too.

She picked up the earpiece and in seconds had an army

of ants moving the sugar cubes…but she didn't stop there. Ants swarmed through the dining room. Columns marched up the wall, covering the chandelier and dimming the room. Scott got nervous. What was she going to do next? Her anger was kind of running away with her.

"Hope!" Pym barked.

She blinked and looked from Scott to Hank as if to say, *See? I'm better at this than either of you.* Then she started walking toward the door. On the way she stopped next to Pym and said, "I don't know why I came to you in the first place."

After she was gone, Pym was silent for a long moment. Then he said, "We can't do this without her."

Scott decided someone had to do something, and it wasn't going to be either of them. That meant it had to be him.

"Oh, God," she said when he found her sitting in her car, and got in. She was in the middle of removing the earpiece she'd used to control the ants.

"You gotta lock your doors," he said, trying to break

the ice. "I mean, really. There's some weird folks in this neighborhood."

"Do you think this is a joke?" she snapped. "Do you have any idea what he's asking you to risk? You have a daughter."

"I'm doing this for her," Scott said. Didn't she already know that?

"You know when my mother died I didn't see him for two weeks?"

"He was in grief."

"Yeah, so was I, and I was seven. And he never came back, not in any way that counted. He just sent me off to boarding school." *Ouch*, Scott thought. "You know, I thought with all that's at stake, just maybe we might have a chance at making peace. But even now he still wants to shut me out."

That's where she was wrong, and Scott needed her to know it. Pym was right. They weren't going to get this job done without Hope, and she wasn't going to be able to help them if she couldn't get some kind of handle on the reasons for why her father did what he did. "He doesn't want to shut you out. He trusts you."

"Then why are you here?" she scoffed.

"It proves that he loves you." He wasn't getting through to her. She looked away. "Hope," he said, trying one last time. "Look at me. I'm expendable. That's why I'm here. You must've realized that by now. I mean, that's why I'm in the suit and you're not. He'd rather lose the fight than lose you."

That was it. That's all he could do. Pym was a jerk, and he'd never be a Father of the Year candidate, but he was trying to protect Hope now. Maybe make up for lost time a little. If she didn't see it... "Anyway," he said, and started to open the car door.

"You know, I didn't know you had a daughter when I called the cops on you," she said. Scott had the feeling there was an apology in there somewhere. "What's her name?"

"Cassie."

"It's a pretty name." Okay. Now they were getting somewhere. They might even start to develop a rapport that didn't involve her beating him up in the martial arts drills. "You have to clear your mind, Scott. You have to make your thoughts precise. That's how it works." She handed him the earpiece. "Think about Cassie, about how badly you want to see her, and use that to focus."

Scott closed his eyes and concentrated. Nothing.

"Open your eyes," she said. "And just think about what you want the ants to do."

He did. Hope had put a penny on the dashboard. *Just think,* Scott told himself. He let his mind wander out, looking for the ants, and some of them appeared around the penny. Two of them picked it up and held it on end. *Hey,* Scott thought. *I'm doing it!*

"Good," she said. For the first time since he'd known her, she had a real smile on her face.

He felt so good about it that he had the ants spin the penny like a top. Just for fun.

CHAPTER 13

Later that afternoon, Pym asked Scott and Hope to come into his study. He was standing, looking at some pictures on the shelves when they got there. "Your mother convinced me to let her join me on my missions," he said. "They called her the Wasp. She was born to it. And there's not a day that goes by that I don't regret having said yes." Hope walked toward him, hearing for the first time the truth she'd always wanted to know.

"It was 1987. Separatists had hijacked a Soviet missile

silo in Kursk and launched an ICBM at the United States. The only way to the internal mechanics was through solid titanium. I knew I had to shrink between the molecules to disarm the missile, but my regulator had sustained too much damage." Pym paused, reliving the events in his mind. There was wonder and admiration on his face—sadness, too—as he went on. "Your mother, she didn't hesitate. She turned off her regulator and went subatomic to deactivate the bomb. She was gone."

Pym turned to his daughter, who had barely moved a muscle while he told the story. "Your mom died a hero," he told her. "And I spent the next ten years trying to learn all I could about the quantum realm."

"You were trying to bring her back." There were tears in Hope's eyes.

Pym slumped a little. "But all I learned was we know nothing." It wouldn't bring back the lost time, Scott knew, but they were starting to understand each other. He hadn't abandoned his daughter; Pym had spent her childhood trying to find her mother, who had saved the United States from a nuclear bomb.

"It's not your fault," Hope said. "She made her choice. But why didn't you tell me this sooner?" she asked, and really started to cry.

"I was trying to protect you. I lost your mother. I didn't mean to lose you, too."

"I'm sorry," Hope whispered.

Scott broke the silence. "This is awesome. It's awesome. Y'know. You guys are breaking down walls, you're healing. It's important." Scott saw the way they were both looking at him and wished he hadn't said anything. "I ruined the moment, didn't I?"

"Yes, you did, yes," Pym said.

Scott could tell they needed some alone time. "I'm going to make some tea," he said.

Later that day Scott made the dive through the keyhole in the doorknob for the first time.

Over the next couple of days, Pym worked feverishly, creating and miniaturizing the gear that the ants would need to overload and disable the lab's power and security systems. Scott spent every waking moment with the ants, learning what they could and couldn't do. He got to know Ant-thony better than the rest of them, since Ant-thony was going to be his main ride in and out of the lab. He ran with the ants, taught them how to build things, learned their little behaviors, and figured out how they worked together.

Then he was ready for the last test before the real show.

"The final phase of your training will be a stealth incursion," Pym said. He showed Scott a schematic drawing. "We must retrieve this prototype of a signal decoy. It's a device that I invented from my S.H.I.E.L.D. days. We need it to counteract the transmission blockers that Cross installed in the Futures vault. It's currently collecting dust in one of Howard Stark's old storage facilities in upstate New York." He showed Scott the map. "Should be a piece of cake."

CHAPTER 14

The next morning, Scott was shivering in the Ant-Man suit, plastered into the back of a crevice in the fuselage of a jet plane on its way from San Francisco to Boston. "It's freezing!" he shouted into the mic. "You couldn't make a simple flannel lining?"

"You're over the target area," Pym said, ignoring Scott's complaints. "Disengage now, Scott."

Scott had his carpenter ants in three groups. "Squadron A, go," he said. The first rank tumbled out into the slipstream. "B, go. C, go." When they were all in the air,

Scott guided Ant-thony toward the edge. "All right, Ant-thony, please don't drop me this time."

Then Ant-thony leaped out into the air, twenty thousand feet above the ground. "Aaaaahhh, it feels like a big leap from sugar cubes to this!" Scott yelled.

"Stay calm," Pym said.

A minute later, when the ants came down through the lowest layer of clouds, Scott said, "Uh, guys, we might have a problem. Hank, didn't you say this was some old warehouse? It's not!"

The old Stark Technologies warehouse in Hank's photographs was now a gleaming new complex with the unmistakable Avengers logo a hundred feet wide on the roof.

"Scott, get out of there," Hope said.

Pym chimed in. "Abort! Abort now."

"No, it's okay," Scott said. He was closer now, and didn't see any lights on or any sign of human—especially Avenger—presence. "It doesn't look like anyone's home. Ant-thony, get me to the roof."

"He's going to lose the suit," Pym said, worried.

Hope looked at him like she couldn't believe that was his biggest problem. "He's going to lose his life," she said.

Ant-thony dropped Scott a foot or so from the gravel rooftop and he tumbled over, hopping to his feet. "All right, I'm on the roof of the target building."

Back in Pym's house, he and Hope saw a shadow flash across one of the monitors feeding them the ant's-eye view. "Somebody's home, Scott."

Almost as soon as he'd spoken, certified Avenger Falcon swooped down and landed on the rooftop not twenty feet from where Scott stood in the gravel. He heard someone talking to Falcon over a microphone in his suit. "What's going on down there, Sam?"

Man, Scott couldn't believe it. He was right there with the Avengers! "It's the Falcon!" he reported to Hope and Pym.

"I had a sensor trip, but I'm not seeing anything," Falcon said, scanning the area to make sure. Looking right at Scott, he said, "Wait a second."

"Abort, Scott," Pym said. "Abort now."

Scott held still, and anyway he was barely the size of the tiny pebbles he stood among. "It's okay. He can't see me."

"I can see you," the Falcon said.

"He can see me." There was only one thing to do. Scott

hit the thumb button and returned to normal size. He popped up the visor on the helmet and said, "Hi. I'm Scott."

Hope turned to her father. "Did he just say, 'Hi, I'm Scott?'" Pym couldn't look her in the eye.

"What are you doing here?" the Falcon asked, all business.

"First off, I'm a big fan," Scott said.

"Appreciate it. So who are you?"

"I'm Ant-Man."

The Falcon tried not to laugh. "Ant-Man?"

"What, you haven't heard of me?" Scott was trying to be cool, but then he reconsidered. "Nah, you wouldn't have heard of me."

"You want to tell me what you want?"

Might as well tell the truth, Scott thought. "I was hoping I could grab a piece of technology just for a few days and return it," he said. "I need it to save the world. You know how that is."

"I know exactly how that is," Falcon said. He started walking toward Scott and talking into his wrist comm. "Located the breach. Bringing him in."

Oh, I don't like this, Scott thought. "Sorry about this," he said, and shrank. Then he launched himself up and punched the Falcon square on the point of his chin. The Falcon reeled backward and took off, the wash from his wings knocking Scott over the edge of the building. Scott hit the grass and took off running.

"What are you doing?" Pym was shouting in his ear.

"Breach is an adult male who has some sort of shrinking tech," Falcon reported as he glided over the lawn where Scott was trying to evade him. He spotted Scott and landed, trying to stomp him. Scott jumped out of the way and buzzed around Falcon's head, throwing punches that he hoped weren't too hard. Or not hard enough. "Sorry about that," he kept saying. Falcon tried to shoot him, but for one thing Scott was too small, and for another he hung on to the gun's barrel sight until Falcon gave up. Then Scott tried to hit him again. This time Falcon saw him coming and threw a punch in time to knock Scott sprawling. Also, he accidentally returned to full-size.

"That's enough!" Falcon said, hauling Scott to his feet—but Scott went after him, putting Hope's moves to good use. He was standing toe-to-toe with one of the Avengers! All of a sudden having the suit was great.

Then Falcon's wings smacked together on either side of Scott's head, and Scott saw stars. He shrank again and shouted, "Ant-thony! A little help?"

Ant-thony appeared, Scott jumped on his back, and they buzzed away toward the warehouse. Falcon followed, but Scott got there first. That meant that when Falcon came in, Scott could again use his size to his advantage. He waited until Falcon stalked through the warehouse door, then he snuck inside Falcon's suit and started tearing at the electronics.

Falcon launched himself backward through the door, spiraling crazily in the air as his wings shorted out. He hit the ground hard, plowing up a furrow for several yards, then leaped to his feet and looked around. But Scott was on his-back, and all he had to do was wait for Ant-thony to catch up.

As he rode Ant-thony away, he heard Falcon saying into his wrist comm, "It's really important to me that Cap never finds out about this."

CHAPTER 15

Scott had sort of thought Pym would admire his guts, but when he got back to San Francisco, he found out just the opposite. "That was completely irresponsible and dangerous!" Pym raged as soon as Scott had gotten back to his house and made it into the kitchen. "You jeopardized everything!"

Scott didn't say a word. He just reached into his back pocket and got the signal device, putting it down on the butcher block table like he was laying down a winning poker hand.

"You got it," Hope said.

Pym, looking amazed, said, "Well done."

"Wait a minute," Scott said. "Did you just compliment me?" He turned to Hope. "He did, didn't he?"

"Kinda sounded like he did," she agreed with a grin.

Pym was examining the signal device, admiring its design. "I was good, wasn't I?" he asked. They all knew it was a rhetorical question.

"Hey, how about the fact that I fought an Avenger and didn't die?" Scott said. He felt like that hadn't been acknowledged quite enough.

"Now let's not dwell on the past," said Hank Pym, who had just been doing exactly that. "We have to finish our planning." He headed for the lab.

"Don't mind him," Hope said. "You did good."

Scott was starting to like her.

Hank Pym opened the door to the living room and stopped short when he saw Darren Cross standing there. "Darren!" he said, making sure Scott and Hope heard him. "How did you get in here?"

"You left the front door open, Hank," Cross said with a grin. "It's official. You're old."

In the kitchen, Hope leaned close to Scott. "The plans!" she whispered. "He will kill him."

The plans for the Pym Tech Futures Lab were lying open on the coffee table. If Cross had seen them...well, Hope was probably right.

But maybe he hadn't seen them yet. Scott got the earpiece in and slipped up to the edge of the door frame.

"Well, to what do I owe this pleasure?"

"I have good news," Cross said, approaching Pym.

"Really? What's that?"

"Pym Tech, the company you created, is about to become one of the most profitable operations in the world. We're anticipating fifteen billion in sales tomorrow alone." While Cross spoke, a group of ants quietly rolled up the plans so all that showed was blank paper. They could have been any set of drawings. Nothing about them would draw attention...unless Cross had already noticed them.

Pym was so focused on the ants for a moment that

what Cross had said didn't register right away. Cross looked a little nonplussed when Pym didn't say anything. He glanced over at the rolled-up plans as the ants accidentally bumped them into a candlestick, but then he turned his attention back to Pym.

"You're welcome," he said. "I know this is odd, but I'd like you to be there. This is my moment; I want you to see it."

"Sure, Darren," Hank said. "Yeah, sure. I'll be there."

Cross nodded, satisfied. Then something else occurred to him. "What did you see in me?" he asked.

"I don't know what you mean," Hank said.

"All those years ago, you picked me. What did you see?"

"I saw myself," Hank said. It was true. Darren Cross had been brash, headstrong, arrogant, and brilliant...just like the young Hank Pym.

"Then why did you push me away?" Cross asked, his voice thick with emotion.

Holding his gaze, Hank Pym delivered the hard truth. "Because I saw too much of myself."

Cross turned and left without another word.

Hope was convinced Cross had seen the plans and was plotting something. "He knows!" she said as soon as Hank came back into the kitchen. "He's baiting you. We have to call it off."

"We're all taking risks," Pym said.

"What if he saw me here?" she asked. Then he would know for sure that she was feeding Hank inside information about the Futures project.

"He didn't," Pym said. "There's no way." Cross hadn't looked into the kitchen. He was sure of it.

"How do you know that?" Hope's phone rang. It was Darren Cross. She gave them all a look as she answered. "Darren, hi."

"Hope." He was in his car, driving. "Where are you right now?"

"I'm at home. Why?"

"I just saw Hank. I still get nothing but contempt from him," Cross said, furious.

"Don't let him rile you up," Hope said. "He's just…he's a senile old man." Scott and Hank exchanged a look at this.

"We need to start everyone working around the clock, get the assembly line up and running. And I'm tripling security. Full sensors at all entrances, and exterior air vents fitted with steel micro-mesh." Cross was edging toward the kind of mania he got when he was close to achieving a goal. Hope had seen it before. She knew her father had, too.

"Great," she said. "Good idea."

"Thank you, Hope. I'm so lucky to have you on my team."

When Darren hung up, she turned back to Scott and her father. "He's tripling security, he's lost his mind, and he's on to you."

"But he's not on to you," Hank said.

She couldn't believe he was being so stubborn when the operation was clearly blown. "He's adding full-body scanners to all entrances and closing exterior vents. How are we going to get Scott inside?"

Buildings needed air, electricity...and water. Those were what connected them to the outside world. Electricity was no help, and if the air vents were blocked, that left... "The water main," Scott said. "You can't add security to a water main. The pressure is too strong, but if we can decrease it, that's how I get in."

Thinking hard, Hope said, "Somebody would have to reach the building's control center to change the water pressure. I mean, Hank and I will be beside Cross. How are we supposed to do that?"

"So we expand our team. What do we need? A fake security guard on the inside to depressurize the water system, somebody else to hack into the power supply and kill the laser grid, and a getaway guy." Three extra guys. Scott thought he knew where he might be able to find them.

Clearly, so did Hank Pym. "No, no, no," he said. "Not those three wombats. No way."

CHAPTER 16

But Hank Pym could see the reality of the situation as well as anyone else, so an hour later Luis, Dave, and Kurt were arranged around the blueprints in the living room as Hope set mugs of coffee in front of them. "Thank you for the coffee, ma'am," Luis said. A thought occurred to him. "It's not too often that you rob a place, and then get welcomed back. Because we just robbed you!" He had a big grin on his face.

"You know that he was arrested for stealing a smoothie machine, right?" Hope asked Scott.

"Two smoothie machines," Luis corrected her.

This did not change her opinion. "Are you sure they can handle this?"

"Oh, we can handle it. We're professionals," Luis said.

"You'll forgive us if we're not instilled with confidence," Pym said. He was standing a little apart from them, watching and appraising.

"Wait, everybody, just kick back and relax a little bit, man," Dave said. "We know our business. We broke into this spooky house, didn't we?"

"I let you," Pym pointed out.

"Well, one could say that I let you let me," Dave said, trying to save face.

"Look, it's okay," Scott said. He knew these guys. They were good. "They can handle this."

"Yeah, we can handle it."

"You got their credentials?" Scott asked Hope.

"He's in the system," she said, meaning she'd added him to Pym Tech's employee database. Luis was going to be their security guard.

"I'm in the system?" Luis looked thrilled.

Dave pointed a you-da-man finger at him. "The system!"

"The system!" Luis said again.

"Yeah," Hank Pym sighed. "We're doomed."

"All right," Scott said, getting down to business. "There's something you guys need to see." He turned and walked out of the room.

Hank was briefing them about the layout when Scott came back wearing the Ant-Man suit. "When you get to this corner," he was saying, "there's gonna be three offices on your left side..."

"That's so cool, bro!" Luis said when he saw Scott in the suit.

"Now, look," Scott said. "This is gonna get weird, all right? It's pretty freaky, but it's safe. There's no reason to be scared."

"Aw, no, Daddy don't get scared," Luis said.

"Really?" This was going to be good, Scott thought. "Good."

He flipped the mask down and shrank.

All three of the thieves shouted. Kurt, looking around the room, said, "This is the work of the gypsies."

"That's—that's—that's witchcraft," Dave echoed.

"Oh, that's amazing," Luis said. "That's like some David Copperfield stuff. That's some kind of wizardry."

"Sorcery!" Kurt cried out.

Luis was still looking around the room, like he was just about to figure out the trick. "How'd you do that, bro?"

"Don't freak out," Scott said. "Look at your shoulder."

Luis did. When he saw miniature Scott, he started screaming and ran out of the room. "I thought Daddy didn't get scared!" Scott said, enjoying every second.

An hour later, the three thieves were snoring in chairs. "I gave them each half a Xanax and Hank explained the science of the suit to them," she explained. Scott had been working on the suit. "Fell right asleep."

She walked Scott to his bedroom—hopefully not still full of bullet ants—and he stopped by the door to get something off his chest. "Hey, look. I want to thank you for—"

"No," she said. "Please don't. We're all doing this for reasons much bigger than any one of us. I'm just glad that you might have a slight chance of maybe pulling this off."

"Hey. Thank you, you know, for that pep talk," he said.

She smiled despite herself. "You know, the honest truth is I actually went from despising you to almost liking you."

"You really should write poetry," he marveled.

"Get some sleep, Scott," she said, and walked away down the hall.

Scott couldn't sleep thinking about the job to come and the dangers of it...and the real possibility that he would never see Cassie again. After lying in bed staring at the ceiling for a while, he made a decision.

Cassie was sleeping when he came into her room and returned to full-size. He wanted more than anything to let her know he was there, to let her know that he loved her more than anyone else in the world, that he was doing this so he could get clear of his old life and be with her again. But he couldn't. All he could do was lean in and kiss her gently on the forehead, and then shrink again and disappear, hoping that wasn't the last time he ever saw her.

He was back at Pym's house in an hour, and after that he slept like a baby.

CHAPTER 17

In the morning, the final skull sessions before the operation started early. Gathered in Pym's lab, Scott ran them through it one more time. "All right, just so we're clear, everyone here knows their role, right? Dave?"

"Wheels on the ground."

"Kurt?"

"Eyes in the sky."

"Luis?"

"Aw, man, you know it. You know what, I get to wear a uniform, that's what's up."

This really wasn't the time for Luis to be a goofball, Scott thought. "Luis," he said again.

Luis looked embarrassed. "I'm sorry, I mean, I'm good, I'm good. I'm just excited, and plus your girlfriend's really hot, so you know that makes me nervous, too, and you are very beautiful, ma'am."

"Oh my lord," Pym said.

"She's not my—" Scott started to say, but he gave up, because once Luis got started there was no stopping him.

"Hey, you know what, I was thinking of a tactic, like when I go undercover, like a whistling, y'know, I'm saying, to like, blend in." Luis looked pleased with himself.

"No," Scott said. "Don't whistle. No whistling, it's not the *Andy Griffith Show*. No whistling."

Luis looked crestfallen, but hey, this was serious business.

That night, the first thing the group did was get Dave and Kurt set up in the van. They disguised it as a utility worker's vehicle, parked it down the street, and put construction cones around it like it was a job site. The reception where Darren Cross planned to announce the Yellowjacket project was crawling with two things: rich people in suits and armed security guards. One of them was Luis, who cleared security, got his badge and gun back, and headed to his position. As soon as Kurt got confirmation of this, he turned to Scott. "We're set."

Scott nodded. "Wish me luck," he said. Then he opened the van's sliding door and as he stepped out over the storm drain, he shrank and fell through the grate.

Luis, whistling a children's tune, swiped his badge and went into the utility control room, keeping himself super casual. But he hadn't expected anyone else to be in there.

"Hey," another guard said, turning away from one of the control panels. "What are you doing?"

"Uh, boss man said to secure the area, so I'm securing," Luis said while he tried to think of what to do next.

The man stepped up on him. "I'm the boss."

"Oh!" That put a little different spin on things, Luis thought.

The guard got out a walkie-talkie. "Utilities workroom three," he said, but he didn't get any further than that, because Luis knocked him out with one punch.

When he'd told Scott he was the only guy ever to knock Peachy out, he wasn't kidding.

With the guard down, Luis got to work. He was part of a team that was saving the world, man, and he had to act like it. Remembering the layout the old guy had shown him, he found the valve controlling the flow in the water main that fed the building and started cranking it.

"Water level is dropping," Kurt said in Scott's ear, but Scott already knew that because he was riding a raft of fire ants through the water main toward the building, and he had more head room than when he'd started. Antthony rode next to him.

"Whoa!" he said as the pipe turned straight down before leveling out again. Just as he got his balance again, Kurt said, "Coming up on extraction pipe."

"I see it! All right, come on, I gotta get up there." The fire ants reconfigured themselves into a kind of ladder and hoisted him up—and other ants in the extraction pipe formed a chain reaching down. They had to time it perfectly or the water would carry them past the extraction pipe, and there was no way Scott could get back upstream. "That's it! That's it, guys, yeah!" Scott encouraged them.

When the two columns of ants met, he swung up into the mouth of the pipe. "Yes! You got it! Come on!" He climbed the fire ant ladder up into Pym Tech's interior plumbing, Ant-thony right behind him. A minute later he popped out in a sink.

"All right, let's fly, Ant-thony," he said. All the carpenter ants moved out, heading for an air vent.

"The Ant-Man is in the building," Kurt reported.

Dave nodded. "Pym's pulling up, right on time." He watched Pym's car...and then noticed another car that had parked nearby when he wasn't watching. He sucked in a breath. "Got a Crown Vic right outside of here."

"This is problem?" Kurt asked.

"Considering the Crown Vic's the most commonly used car for undercover cops, man, yes, this is a problem."

Dave watched as two cops jumped out of the car and headed after Pym. "Oh no," he said. This was a complication they did not need.

Inside, Scott moved to help out Luis. "I'm employing

the bullet ants," Scott said, knowing that Luis and Hope would be in position. *"Hapanera-clamda-mana-merna.* I don't remember what it's called, but I feel bad for this guy."

The bullet ants dropped out of the air vent onto the shoulders of the guard manning the entrance to the lab. As Luis strolled in the guard's direction, the ants attacked and he started to jump around, yelling in pain. Luis took a big step forward and decked him. One punch and out, just like the plan.

"See, that's what I'm talkin' 'bout, that's what I call it, an unfortunate casualty, in a very serious operation," he said as Hope walked by him and swiped her way into the lab.

She didn't waste any time. Walking purposefully right to the server rack, she inserted the signal device into the rack and slid it shut. Meanwhile Luis dragged the unconscious guard into the server space where nobody would see him.

"Signal decoy in place," Kurt reported as he saw it come online. "Mean pretty lady did good, Scott."

Dave peered through binoculars at the cops who had stopped Pym before he could go inside the building. "Looks like Pym's getting arrested," he said.

"Scott, we have problem," Kurt called out.

"Problem? What's the problem?"

Before Kurt could answer, Dave opened the door and headed across the street. "Dave! Dave, that's not part of plan!" Kurt yelled after him, but Dave was on a mission.

"Listen to me," Hank said to the two cops. "If I don't get into this building people will die."

"That's awfully dramatic," Gale said. He didn't believe a word of it. They had some questions for Pym, and they didn't care about his reception.

Their questions were interrupted in the nick of time for Hank, when Dave hopped into the Crown Vic, turned on the lights and sirens, and squealed away.

"Are you kidding me?" Paxton couldn't believe it. He and Gale took off after their car, while Pym took advantage of the diversion and got himself inside.

Observing from the van, Kurt said, "Problem solved."

CHAPTER 18

Hope came out of the lab with Luis close behind her—only now he was wearing the unconscious guard's uniform so he could be in the lab without drawing notice. As they came out, they saw Darren Cross standing in the hallway like he'd been waiting for them. "Well," he said.

Hope had an anxious moment. How much had he seen? If he found out about the plan now, people were going to die.

But after a long pause, all Darren said was, "How do I look?"

She tried not to show how relieved she was as Darren walked her out to the lobby, where Hank was just coming through security. "There he is, just in time," Darren said. "Come on."

He led them to the lab, to the chamber containing the Yellowjacket pod. It was protected by a retinal scanner. "Twelve-point verification," the scanner said after Cross put his eye up to the screen. "Confirming authorization."

"Little over the top, don't you think, Darren?" Hank said.

Darren didn't seem offended. "No, you can never be too safe," he said.

The computer voice in the scanner said, "Access granted," and the door opened. Cross, Pym, and Hope walked in, with Cross's bodyguards behind them.

"I want to hand it to you, Darren; you really did it," Hank said. The Yellowjacket project really was impressive.

"And you only know the half of it, Hank."

The door closed behind them.

"Arriving at second position," Scott said. "All right, top speed, Ant-thony. Let's go. Proceeding to command position."

Thousands of crazy ants were flooding over the servers that held all of Pym Tech's backup information. It had to be destroyed or even if they got the Yellowjacket suit, Cross could just build another one. Also they had to knock the power out for a few seconds, and the crazy ants would do that, too...if it worked. *Time to find out*, Scott thought.

"I'll be right back, Ant-thony," he said, hopping off the ant onto the top of one of the frames holding the delicate electronics. "All right, guys, I'm in position. I'm going to signal the ants."

Outside, Paxton and Gale were looking at their crashed car while Dave threw himself back into the van, laughing. "Did you see that?"

Then he accidentally hit the horn, and over by the wrecked Crown Vic, Paxton looked up. He remembered that horn.

"Assume formation," Scott said. The crazy ants lined themselves up, spread all the way across the huge server farm. Each of them had a small conducting amplifier on its back, to enhance their natural ability to conduct electricity without harming themselves. "All right, you cute little crazies," Scott said. "Let's fry these servers."

Electricity crackled across the room and thousands of miniature lightning bolts shot from server to server, scrambling the magnetic patterns holding the data. Scott whooped. It was working!

"Let's go get it, buddy!" he shouted, and Ant-thony was there to carry him off to the next objective.

"Servers are fried," Kurt reported from the van. "Data backup completely erased."

Right on, Scott thought. "Headed to the particle chamber," he answered.

Now it was really showtime.

Pym got a cold feeling in the pit of his stomach when he saw Mitchell Carson and his retinue enter the Yellowjacket chamber. Carson glanced at Pym and then shook hands with Darren. "Hello, Dr. Cross. My associates agree to your terms."

"Wonderful," Cross said. Seeing the expression on Hank's face, he got a smug grin on his own. "Mr. Carson introduced me to these fine gentlemen here. They're representatives of Hydra." Knowing Hank's history with S.H.I.E.L.D., mortal enemy of Hydra, he explained a little more. "They're not what they were. They're doing some interesting work. And I'm enjoying myself."

Cross stepped to Hank and now he really started to gloat. This was why he had wanted Hank here. Not to celebrate, but so Cross could rub Hank's face in what Cross was about to do. "You tried to hide your technology from me," he said, "and now it's going to blow up in your face."

Hank hauled off and punched him. Cross flinched back and bent over, one hand on the side of his jaw, but when he stood up again, he didn't look angry at all. "Wow," he said, and gave Hank an admiring nod. "Wow! I mean, I saw the punch coming a mile away, but I just figured it'd be all pathetic and weak."

"Well, you figured wrong," Pym said. And in the next couple of minutes, they would all find out whether Scott Lang had figured wrong, too.

Paxton nodded as he walked to the van. "I know this van." Lang had been driving it at Cassie's birthday party. What the hell was going on? He pounded on the door. "Anybody home?"

Inside, Kurt and Dave huddled, hoping the cops would give up and go away before Scott needed them again.

"All right, guys, I'm here," Scott said from inside the particle chamber. "Setting the charges." Several dozen fire ants carrying miniature explosive charges touched buttons that returned the charges to regular size. This chamber contained all the reserves of the miniaturization fluid that gave the Yellowjacket suit its powers. Like the backup data, it had to be destroyed to put a permanent end to Cross's project. The timers on each charge read *15:00...14:59...*

"Great job, guys," Scott said. "I'll take it from here." Carpenter ants picked up loads of the smaller fire ants and crazy ants, swooping away to return home. Now all Scott had left were the few bullet ants and carpenter ants he would need for the last phase of the operation. He stood at the top of the tiny injection pipe that led down into the Yellowjacket pod.

"Final position," he said, and dropped a miniaturized screw down the pipe as a test. It pinged off the side and then was vaporized at the bottom. The laser defenses were still intact, which meant Kurt hadn't gotten the power down yet. "Guys? How we lookin' on that laser grid?"

"Almost!" Kurt said.

Dave shook his head. "No, you're not."

"I'm getting close!"

"No, you're not."

"San Francisco PD!" a cop shouted from outside. They

were banging on the doors still. "Man in the van! I know you're in there!"

"Make it go faster," Dave hissed.

"Dude," Kurt hissed back. "Seriously."

Scott had himself harnessed to a line at the top of the injection tube. "Ready to jump," he said. "Do you read, Kurt?" He really couldn't wait any longer.

"So close..." Kurt couldn't take his eyes off the status bar. Ninety percent there...the laser grid would go out any second.

The cops yanked the back doors of the van open, guns drawn. "Freeze!" they shouted.

Dave started talking to delay them. "Okay! Wait a minute, wait a minute! There was a guy that looked exactly like me who attacked us and put us in the back of this disgusting van."

"Get out," one of the cops said. He hauled Dave out and threw him facedown on the pavement.

"Take it easy!" Dave protested.

The status bar hit one hundred percent.

"Go! Go now!" Kurt said as he was hauled out of the van behind Dave. But he had to hit the space bar to execute the hack, and the cop had gotten to him before he could. "Wait!"

Scott was already falling down the tube. "What? What do you mean, wait?" he screamed. He fell toward the laser grid, and there was nothing he could do about it— he was about to be vaporized. Cross would sell his tech to someone evil and take over the world. More important, Scott would never see Cassie again.

Kurt fought the cop who was manhandling him out of the van. With a last desperate lunge he got a finger on the space bar and the program executed. With a sigh of relief he let the cop drag him away ... and inside the tube, the laser grid flickered out just as Scott fell through the mouth of the tube!

He'd made it into the Yellowjacket pod.

CHAPTER 19

But the Yellowjacket suit wasn't there! The pod was empty, and a port in the bottom of it was just irising shut. "What? What?" Scott looked around, dangling at the end of the line.

There was a knock at the window. "Hey, little guy," Darren Cross said. He chuckled and held up a tiny glass case holding the Yellowjacket suit.

"Oh sh—gah!" The laser grid came back on and cut the line. Scott fell to the bottom of the pod chamber with a thump.

Outside, Cross turned away from the pod, reveling in the way he'd outsmarted the mighty Hank Pym.

"I always suspected you had a suit stored away somewhere," he said, playing to the room. "Which begs the question: Who is the new Ant-Man? Who is the man that my beloved mentor trusted even more than me?"

Screens in the room flickered to life, displaying Scott's mug shot from when he'd been arrested after the Vista job went wrong. "Scott Lang," Cross said. "The martyr. He took on the system and paid the price, losing his family and his only daughter in the process. Exactly your kind of guy, Hank."

The screen now showed a picture of Cassie. Scott scrambled to the window, frantically trying to figure out how he could escape. He threw himself against the glass, but it held.

Cross put the Yellowjacket suit in a secure padded case and continued his story. "He escapes his jail cell without leaving any clue as to how, and then he disappears magically, despite having no money to his name, and now he brings me the Ant-Man suit, the only thing that can rival my creation." Cross had a look on his face like a man who had just won the lottery without even knowing he had entered.

"Darren, don't do this," Pym said. "If you sell to these men, it's going to be chaos."

"I already have, and for twice the price, thanks to you," Cross said. "It's not easy to successfully infiltrate an Avengers facility. Thankfully, word travels fast. Oh, I'll sell them the Yellowjacket, but I'm keeping the particle to myself."

Mitchell Carson's head snapped around. Apparently this was news to him.

"They don't run on diesel," Cross said to Carson. "If you want the fuel, you'll have to come to me." Cross handed the vial of Yellowjacket fluid to one of his bodyguards, looking back to Pym. "What do you call the only man who can arm the most powerful weapon in the world?"

"The most powerful man in the world," Hank said, because he knew that's what Cross wanted to hear. He was trying to keep Cross talking while he figured out some way to stop him.

Cross nodded. "You proud of me yet?"

Hank wasn't going to give him that satisfaction. "You can stop this, Darren. It's not too late."

"It's been too late for a long time now," Cross said, and his bodyguards drew their guns.

"Darren!" Hope said. "What are you doing?"

"He wasn't any more capable of caring for you than he was for me," Cross said to her. Now he was dead serious.

"This is not who you are," she said. "It's the particles altering your brain chemistry."

He seemed to think about this for a moment. Then he waved his arms. "Wait, wait, wait, wait, wait, wait, wait. You're right." He held out a hand for one of the bodyguards' guns. "I have to be the one to do it."

That was the last straw. As Cross leveled the gun at Hank Pym, Hope snapped an elbow back into the face of the nearest guard and ripped the gun from his hand as he fell. She pointed it at Cross.

It was a standoff.

"Here we go," said Mitchell Carson as he backed away so he wasn't in anyone's line of fire.

"Drop your gun," Hope said to Cross, biting off each word.

"You know, I came to the house the other night to kill him, but you were there," Cross said. He didn't drop his gun.

"You're sick and I can help you," she replied. Her voice shook, but her hands were steady. "Just put the gun down."

"I wasn't ready to kill you then. But I think I am now!" Cross was lost in full-blown madness. Whether it was the Yellowjacket particles or not—whatever the cause—he'd completely lost it.

"Drop your gun now!"

"You picked the wrong side, Hope." Cross's finger tightened on the trigger.

Inside the pod chamber, Scott realized he still had an option. The discs. He hadn't used them. He got the blue one out. Blue for enlarging.

He threw the disc at the window. When it made contact, it forcibly expanded the distance between the atoms of the window, shattering it in a violent explosion. Scott charged through the hole, shrinking as he went. Cross shot at Hank but missed him because the blast of force had pushed him off balance. Gunfire erupted. The bodyguards were shooting at Scott, but they didn't have a chance of hitting him. Hank threw a punch at Cross and grappled for his gun. Another bodyguard attacked

Hope, knocking her gun away. She fought back, landing a couple good hits that took him down.

Another gun went off. Flashing back to full-size, Scott saw Hank fall and land flat on his back with blood leaking from a wound in his shoulder. "Dad!" Hope screamed.

The last guard standing leveled his gun at Hank. Scott shrank again and hit him in the midsection. Before he could recover, Scott grew again and knocked him out with a final shot to the jaw.

"Hank," he said, running over to Pym and flipping up his mask. "Hank. Listen, you're gonna be okay. All right? You're gonna be just fine." The wound looked bad, but maybe not fatal. Hank's eyes were glassy with shock.

Then Scott heard a clink and felt something against the back of his head. He'd forgotten about Darren Cross.

"Take the suit off," Cross said, "or I'll blow your brains out and peel it off."

Scott didn't know what to do...but Hope did. She still had an earpiece, and she could still control the ants. Cross tried to fire his gun, but there were ants blocking the hammer. Bullet ants. A moment later they were all over him, biting for all they were worth. Flailing at them,

Cross grabbed the case containing the Yellowjacket suit and ran... while Mitchell Carson crept up to one of the fallen bodyguards and retrieved the vial of Yellowjacket serum.

Alarms were sounding all through the Pym Tech complex. Cross reached the outer atrium of the lab. Picking off the last of the bullet ants, he issued a series of orders to his waiting men. "Get me to the roof and radio ahead. I want to make sure the helicopter's ready to take off," he said. "You two," he added to a pair of security guards near the vault door, "kill anything that comes out of that vault."

Hope knelt over her father, who was in bad shape. "Can you move?" she asked him. Hank didn't answer.

"We need to get him out of here," Scott said.

Hope turned to him. "Go get that suit," she said. They hadn't gone through all this just to watch Darren Cross get away.

139

CHAPTER 20

Scott raced out of the vault and immediately started dodging bullets. He veered away from the two guards, shrinking and dashing across the resin model of the new Cross Technologies complex. The guards kept firing, their bullets chewing the display to pieces. Scott couldn't dodge them forever—but he didn't have to, because Luis came to the rescue, flying into the room and taking both of the guards out with two hammering right hands. "Hey, Scotty," he said, shaking his sore hand. He couldn't see where Scott had gone. "Hey, did I save your life? Scotty? Scotty?"

Scott appeared, expanding to full-size. "Thank you, Luis," he panted.

"Hey, are we the good guys?" Luis wondered out loud, as if it had just occurred to him.

"Yeah, we're the good guys."

Luis grinned. "Feels kinda weird, you know?"

"Yeah. But we're not done yet." Scott started running again. As he shrank he warned Luis, reminding him of the explosive charges in the particle chamber. "Get out of here before this place blows!"

Luis started running, too...and then he stopped as he passed the server room. "Oh! That guy." He couldn't just leave the security guard lying in there. If he was going to be a good guy, he had to act like one.

He swiped his ID card and started yelling at the unconscious guard. "Hey! We're getting out of here."

Back in the Yellowjacket pod chamber, Hope tried to get her father to his feet. "The charges are set. We've got to find a way out of here and fast."

"Don't worry," Hank said. He was out of breath, but he could sit up...and maybe more. "I'm not going to die. And neither are you." He held up a keychain. Dangling at the end of it was a tiny tank.

Hope looked at her father, who, even in his agony, had a bit of a twinkle in his eye. "It's not a keychain," he said.

Paxton had called in the shots fired when he'd first heard them, and let go of the two lowlifes who had swiped his car. Now everything was spiraling out of control. "Total chaos in here," he radioed in to HQ. "Multiple shots fired."

Above him, something blew the walls out and over the front of Pym Tech's main building. A full-size tank, engine revving, had burst through the wall and crashed down—trailing a giant-sized chain and what looked to Paxton like a key ring. What was going on here?

He had no idea, but he was a good cop, and he radioed it in. "And there's a tank."

The dispatcher asked him to repeat it.

Luis got the security guard out, but he had to detour around the tank to reach the paramedics. "A little help!" He handed the guard off and saw Hope and Hank climbing out of the tank. "I got him," he said, helping Hank walk while Hope called out to another pair of paramedics.

"We need a doctor!" she said. The paramedics took Hank away and Luis looked around, wondering what to do next. Where was Scott? How long did they have before the building blew?

He heard the unmistakable horn of his van right before he saw it swerve into the VIP parking area. Dave and Kurt were still on the job.

On the roof, Cross and his men—and, most important, the Yellowjacket case—were on the helicopter. "Let's go!" he shouted over the rotor wash.

Then he saw a cloud of flying ants coming from the

roof access door. *Lang*, he thought. He pulled out his gun and started firing. He didn't have a great chance of hitting any of them, but who knows? Maybe he would get lucky.

Riding on the faithful Ant-thony, Scott was toward the front of the flying battalion of carpenter ants. Cross's first shots roared by without hitting anything. He kept firing and Scott felt a shock below him. Suddenly he was falling into space. He landed on the back of another carpenter ant a foot below. Looking back he saw one of Ant-thony's wings spiraling down toward the roof.

"Ant-thony!" Scott cried out. A nine-millimeter bullet hitting a carpenter ant... Ant-thony never knew what hit him, Scott thought. He turned back toward the helicopter. Its fuselage door was slamming shut, but Scott could see Darren Cross inside, looking right at him.

"You're going to regret that," he said. The helicopter lifted away, and the ants followed.

Paxton watched the helicopter take off. Following its flight path, he saw the van. The one Lang had driven, and now he knew the two losers inside had something to do with the chaos here because a third guy in a security guard uniform was hopping into the front seat.

"Get out of that van!" Paxton shouted, running toward the van.

"What?" Luis shouted back.

"Get out of that van!"

Luis touched his ear. "It's too loud—there's a tank! I can't hear you!"

Dave gunned the van and they made their getaway, Paxton shouting uselessly after them.

If Darren Cross thought he'd gotten away, he didn't think so for long. The helicopter took a little while to reach full speed, and carpenter ants were faster than most people knew. Scott caught up to it before it was five hundred yards from Pym Tech. He punched a hole through the window and knocked out the first bodyguard.

Cross responded quickly and carelessly. He started shooting at Scott, making more holes in the windows and fuselage of the copter. "Are you crazy? Put the gun down!" one of the other bodyguards yelled. Still trying to track Scott, Cross fired directly at the guard holding the Yellowjacket case. The case saved the guard's life, but the bullet broke it open.

Scott looked down at the Yellowjacket suit. Maybe there was a chance!

Cross saw him and swung the gun up to point it right at Scott. "Did you think you could stop the future with a heist?" he shouted.

"It was never just a heist," Scott shouted back. He saw understanding on Cross's face right as all of the explosive charges inside Pym Tech went off at once.

The explosion blew out every window in the building and started to collapse the upper floors. Then—just as Hank Pym had predicted when they first planned the operation—the Pym Particles did what they did best. Unleashed by the explosives, they shrank the entire Pym Tech building into a tiny glowing point of fire. From a gurney being loaded into an ambulance, Hank watched his life's work disappear—but Darren Cross's crazed plans were also disappearing. They'd done what they had to do.

A moment later the tiny fireball winked out, and Pym Tech was gone as if it had never existed.

Cross kept shooting at Scott until Scott made a mistake. He dodged a bullet and lost his balance. He skidded out under the fuselage door and grew back to full-size, hanging on the outside of the helicopter. He glanced down—the ground was a long way off—and saw the van roaring along the road below them. Dave and Luis and Kurt were still on the job. He'd been right to trust them.

Scott clambered back into the helicopter. He didn't see Darren Cross for a moment...and then, growing into view, the Yellowjacket suit appeared.

Uh-oh, Scott thought. He shrank again and Cross blasted away at him with the Yellowjacket's energy beams, which were mounted on little appendages that stuck up from its shoulders. The beams tore through the helicopter, destroying whatever they touched—and in his frenzy, Cross didn't care when a stray beam fried part of the dashboard between the two pilots in the cockpit.

The helicopter swerved crazily. "Got to set her down somewhere!" one of the pilots shouted. The helicopter started descending as he wrestled to keep control of it.

Scott launched himself at Cross and landed a powerful punch right on the Yellowjacket mask. He bounced off and Cross shrank, rocketing toward him. They traded punches and Cross kept firing energy beams. He didn't hit Scott, but he did manage to hit both pilots. The helicopter went into a spin.

The force of the spin threw both Scott and Cross across the floor and into the open Yellowjacket case. The case slammed shut, and as the helicopter kept tilting, it slid back—and out the open door. They bounced around inside the falling case. Cross's beams kept zapping out.

They shattered a roll of candy into little green pieces. Cross's phone activated as Scott bounced off its home button.

"I'm gonna disintegrate you!" Cross shouted.

They both were flattened by the impact of the padded case as it hit the ground—but it wasn't the ground, they figured out right away. Chlorinated water came pouring in through the holes made by Yellowjacket's beams. They'd landed in a swimming pool.

Cross expanded to full-size, blowing the case apart. The terrified family whose pool they'd landed in started screaming. "Call 911!" the father said, but Yellowjacket disintegrated the table where his phone lay. Scott flashed back to full-size, rising up out of the pool and slamming Cross aside before he could harm the family. Both of them crashed through a patio door and then back out onto the patio. Scott, knocked flat on his back, saw the miniature Cross coming at him ... and he saw a discarded Ping-Pong paddle lying near his hand. So he did what came naturally.

He grabbed the paddle and slapped Yellowjacket out of

the air. Cross hurtled across the back yard and hit a bug zapper hanging from the eaves over the shattered patio door. It crackled violently and then subsided.

Scott turned to the family, who were huddled together by the far end of the pool. "It's okay," he said.

They screamed and ran. Scott looked at the bug zapper, wondering if it had really put an end to Yellowjacket. Then he heard an unwelcome familiar voice. "Police! Put your hands up! Get 'em up!"

He turned around, seeing Paxton and Gale. Scott flipped the Ant-Man mask up so they could see his face. "Scott?" Paxton said in amazement.

Scott was relieved to be talking to a cop he knew. "Paxton. You have to listen to me—"

But Paxton didn't. Instead he zapped Scott with a Taser, dropping him like a sack of potatoes to the pool deck.

CHAPTER 21

cott woke up in the back of Paxton's squad car. The Ant-Man helmet was next to him on the backseat, but he couldn't reach it. "Paxton. Turn around, take me back," he said.

"I am taking you back. To prison."

"There's something in that backyard that needs to be destroyed," Scott said. "In the bug zapper, it—"

Paxton stomped on the brakes and turned to face Scott. "You need to desist right now! Your delusions are out of hand!"

Delusions? Scott thought. *Does he think the suit is a delusion?*

Things might have gotten worse, but the squad car's radio crackled and a dispatcher came on. "All units, we have a two thirty-six in progress at eight-forty Winter Street."

The address registered with both Scott and Paxton at the same time. "Cassie!" Scott said.

Paxton floored it and the squad car squealed away, lights and sirens going. They got to Paxton's house in record time and Paxton brought the car to a rocking halt, opening the door before the car had completely stopped. "Paxton, let me help."

"Don't move," Paxton ordered him as he and Gale got out of the car.

"Let me help!" Scott begged, but Paxton ignored him. He saw Maggie coming toward him from a cluster of other police cars that had also responded. She was frantic. "He's got Cassie!"

"Who's got Cassie?"

"That thing, that thing, I don't know what it is!"

Scott threw himself flat on the backseat. Maybe he

couldn't reach the helmet with his hands, but if he could work his head into it...yes! It worked! The faceplate swung shut, and Scott shrank out of the handcuffs. Then he was out of the car and running toward the house to save his daughter.

Inside Cassie's room, her toy train ran around and around while she sat on the bed trying not to look scared of the man in the yellow-and-black suit. "Are you a monster?" she asked.

"Do I look like a monster?" Cross responded.

"I want my daddy."

Cross nodded. "I want your daddy, too."

She screamed as he picked her up, and at that moment Ant-Man appeared in the room, growing to full-size as he came through the window. "There you are," Cross said with satisfaction.

"Daddy, is that you?"

Scott flipped up the mask. "Hi, peanut," he said, try-ing to keep his voice normal. His heart lifted when she gave him a smile, showing the new gaps in her front teeth. Then Scott looked back to Cross and said, "Why don't you pick on someone your own size?"

Before Cross could respond, Scott hit him with the second of the discs Hank Pym had made. Red for shrinking. Yellowjacket vanished and so did Scott, and Cassie ran into the closet. Scott landed on her train table and started running between the fibers of a little rug Cassie had set there as a play area for her stuffed animals. Cross was on top of the train engine, looking around. "Now where'd you go, little guy...? There you are."

He blasted away at the rug, the Yellowjacket's energy beams hitting it with tiny puffs of smoke. Cassie watched from the closet door.

"Not just me," Scott said as he burst out of the rug— flanked by an army of ants. They swarmed up and over the train, harrying Yellowjacket. That gave Scott time to get onto the train. He picked up the caboose and flung it at Cross, who blew it apart in midair. Scott tried again, with the next-to-last car, with the same result. The ants kept attacking Yellowjacket, sacrificing themselves to give

Scott more time. Scott threw a train bridge at Yellow-jacket, knocking him off and onto the tracks. The train hit him and derailed...but Yellowjacket was unharmed. Scott was keeping him away from Cassie, but he wasn't any closer to putting Yellowjacket out of commission.

Outside, Dave drove the van toward the cop's house. "Scotty needs us, know what I'm sayin'?"

"Ain't nothin' gonna stop us," Luis said as they came down the block—and saw what looked like every cop car in San Francisco blocking the street. A bunch of cops looked at them.

Luis changed his mind. They couldn't help Scotty from jail, now, could they?

"Back it up. Back it up slow," he said.

Dave nodded. "Yeah." He dropped the van in reverse and they went back up the block, hoping none of the cops would recognize them. But still, they wanted to help Scotty. What could they do?

The problem was the Yellowjacket suit could fly and had weapons. That put Scott at a serious disadvantage. How was he going to get around that?

Yellowjacket flew up into the air, barraging Scott with energy blasts. "You insult me, Scott," Cross said. "Your very existence is insulting to me." Getting frustrated because he couldn't get a good bead on Scott, he growled, "You know, it would be much easier to hit you if you were bigger."

This gave Scott an idea. He'd forced Yellowjacket to shrink. He had some of the blue discs left. "Yeah, I agree," he said, and spun one in Cross's direction.

Cross batted it aside and the disc hit one of the bullet ants on the rug. It chittered—and all of a sudden it was the size of a dog. A big dog. *Whoa*, Scott thought. He threw another one and again Cross deflected it. Bam! The train engine expanded, punching out the window and part of the wall of Cassie's bedroom, its painted-on face looking out over the astonished cops in the street with a smile. The train tipped out over the yard and crushed one of the squad cars.

Paxton had seen enough. "Cassie!" he yelled out, and charged into the house and up the stairs.

In Cassie's room, Yellowjacket was blasting apart everything Scott threw at him. "Let me show you just how insignificant you are," he gloated.

As Paxton ran up the stairs, he smacked right into an ant the size of a Saint Bernard. It knocked him back down the stairs and ran outside, chittering the whole way. Gale and Maggie watched it go by. "That's a messed-up-looking dog," Gale said.

"I'm going to destroy everything you love," Cross said, still blasting away at the miniaturized Ant-Man. Then he spun around as Paxton shouted, "Freeze!"

Cross swatted the gun from Paxton's hand and stood, enjoying Paxton's sudden confusion. Scott jumped up on Yellowjacket's back and tried to pry the cover off the blasters' power source. "I can't break through," he said to himself.

But Cross heard. "It's titanium, you idiot." He reached back and squeezed Scott between his palms. Scott flashed to full-size and belted him in the face. "Get her out of here!" he shouted at Paxton. Cassie was hiding behind his legs.

"Come on," Paxton said—but Yellowjacket stepped between them and the door. "Sorry, sweetheart," Cross said, almost gently. "You have to help Daddy pay for his mistakes."

"You stay behind me, okay?" Paxton said. Scott gave him all the credit in the world. He was laying his life on the line for Cassie.

"I'm going to have to shrink between the molecules to get in there," Scott said. He'd always talked to himself while on a job, and it was the same now. He remembered Hank's story about the titanium missile housing, and how Hank's wife had disappeared into the quantum realm to disarm the warhead.

"Daddy, help!" Cassie screamed. Yellowjacket's blasters powered up again.

Leaping toward the power unit on Yellowjacket's back, Scott said, "I love you, Cassie." He punched a button to override the regulator and vanished into the spaces between the titanium atoms. He fell through the power unit, shattering links and circuits on the way. He could hear Cross screaming in frustration as his systems went offline and he lost control of the suit—and then Scott shattered the matrix of Pym Particles at the core of the power unit, and everything changed.

Paxton saw the yellow-and-black armored suit start to crackle and shut down. The man inside thrashed around, trying to get control of it. Then things got even stranger than they already had been. The suit started to crumple in on itself, like all the air was being sucked out of it. It crumpled and shrank, sparks shooting out of it...and then, just like Pym Tech, the entire suit and the man inside shrank into a brilliant glowing speck. It hung in the air for a few seconds, slowly dimming, and then it was gone.

"Daddy, where are you?" Cassie said.

Scott fell through the subatomic realm. He got smaller and smaller. When he'd started falling, he'd seen dust motes the size of houses. Now he was seeing atoms themselves, tracing the patterns of the electrons that orbited each one. Ahead, he thought he could start to see the quantum realm that lay under the material universe. It was…there was no way to describe it, but he was pretty sure that if he got there, it was going to be a one-way trip.

He tried punching buttons to make himself grow again. Nothing happened. "Oh no," he said, remembering more about what Pym had said.

You would enter a reality where all concepts of time and space become irrelevant. And as you shrink…for all eternity…everything that you know…and love…gone forever.

He heard Cassie's voice echoing from somewhere far away.

"Daddy!"

He was becoming part of it. He couldn't turn around, couldn't grow… "Cassie," he said. Still he heard her voice. *"Come on, Daddy…"*

And Pym's voice again: *"Do not mess with the regulator."*

That was it. Scott fumbled at his belt, looking around at the endless emptiness. He still had a blue disc. Blue for expansion. If he could connect it to the regulator…

He popped open the regulator housing. There was no time for fancy engineering. He held the disc in place, forced the housing shut again, and took a deep breath. Then he punched the button to return to normal size.

The entire universe seemed to heave around him. He felt his growth accelerate and go on and on. He wasn't growing or shrinking by a factor of a thousand. He was becoming a billion times bigger, or a trillion.

Cassie's bedroom coalesced around him and Scott dropped to his knees. He'd done it.

"Daddy!" Cassie shouted. She ran to him and jumped into his arms. "I love you so much."

"I love you, too," he said. That was the only important thing. "So much."

Paxton gave them a moment and then he cleared his throat. Scott looked over at him, wondering if he was about to be under arrest again. But Paxton pointed up and said, "There's a big hole in the roof."

Scott looked up, too. There sure was. "Sorry," he said.

When Gale and the SWAT team came pounding up the stairs into Cassie's bedroom, with Maggie right in the middle of them, they found Paxton holding Cassie. "Is she all right?" Maggie asked.

Paxton nodded. "She's fine."

"Mommy," Cassie said. As Paxton handed her over to Maggie, Cassie—and only Cassie—saw the tiny shadow of her father waving good-bye to her from the edge of her nightstand. He leaped away and was gone.

But she knew he would be back.

CHAPTER 22

Scott couldn't wait to tell Hank about what had happened to Darren Cross, and as he'd expected, Hank wanted to hear every word. Then he wanted to hear more about the subatomic journey. "Scott, please. You don't remember anything?"

"Hank, I...I don't." He'd already told Hank that he'd heard Cassie's voice, and something about the discs...but his memory was foggy. Maybe he'd been too small for memories to form or something. He didn't know.

"There must be something else," Hank said. But there

wasn't. Scott didn't have anything else to say to him. Hank sighed. "Well, I suppose the human mind just can't comprehend the experience, but you made it. You went in and you got out. It's amazing."

Scott knew how much this meant to him. If he could go and come back, that meant that maybe there was a chance for Hope's mother to do the same. Maybe she wasn't gone forever. But none of them could say that out loud.

"Scott," Hope said. "I'll walk you out." Scott got the message. Hank was still recovering from his gunshot wound. Hope didn't want him to get too excited.

Scott stood up. "Get some rest," he said, and followed Hope out.

Hank sat, lost in thought. Was it possible? He gazed at an old picture of Janet, taken when Hope was still a baby. Maybe...

He got up, meaning to go down to the lab and putter around while he thought about these new ideas. When he opened the door, though, he found Hope in the middle of a kiss with Scott. "When did this happen?" he asked. He hadn't had any idea.

"Nothing's happening," Hope said.

"Well, hold on. Something's kind of happening," Scott said.

"Well if that's the case, shoot me again," Hank said.

Scott played to the occasion. "Yeah, I don't know what you're doing grabbing me and kissing me like that. I was a little surprised myself. I have to get somewhere. I'll see you later, Hank. Really, Hope." He headed for the stairs, with Hope smiling at him.

"Scott," Hank called as Scott reached the stairs.

"Yeah."

"You're full of it."

"Oh yeah."

Then he was gone, and Hank realized that, at some point during the past few days, he'd rediscovered hope. And Hope. They were a family again.

Later that evening, Scott was over at Paxton and Maggie's house for dinner. They were all making an effort to reconnect. Scott knew he was never going to get together with Maggie again, but he wanted to be part of Cassie's new family, too. "Well, Scott," Paxton said when they were finishing up. "I met with my captain today. He wanted a report of the night you got out of jail." Scott got tense. This was where things might go really wrong. "Something happened with the cameras, and circuits got fried, and..." He shrugged. "But I told him you were processed correctly."

Scott couldn't quite believe this. "Really?" This was a huge favor. Escape would have added years to his sentence, even if Hope decided not to press charges on the original crime that had landed him in jail.

"Well, yeah. Can't be sending Cassie's dad back to jail on a technical glitch, right?"

Scott was now regretting calling Paxton a butthead a couple of weeks back. He was a decent guy, a standup guy, and he was good for Cassie, too. "Thank you, Paxton. I'm blown away. Thank you for everything you do for Cassie."

"Oh, well, that's my pleasure," Paxton said. "But no, this one...I did it for you."

For a moment they almost had a kind of emotional connection. Then both of them noticed it and they looked away from each other. "This is awkward," Scott said.

"Yeah," Paxton agreed.

Cassie chimed in. "Yeah."

"I mean, what do we even talk about after all that?"

"Oh, I know!" Cassie said.

"What?"

"I did my first cartwheel today."

"What?"

Maggie nodded. "Yeah. She has been practicing all week, but today was the magic day."

Paxton reached into his pocket. "I recorded it on my phone. Here."

Sure enough, on the screen, there was Cassie doing cartwheel after cartwheel. "No, that can't be Cassie," Scott said. He turned to her. "That's not you."

"Yeah it is," she said with a gap-toothed grin.

"This is a professional gymnast. There's no way that's her," Scott went on, stringing the joke out. Cassie loved it when he teased her like this.

"Yeah, that's her," both Maggie and Paxton said.

Cassie, meanwhile, was feeding the dog-sized ant under the table. It couldn't stay out in the wild anymore, and it sure was a cool pet to have. "Good boy," she said.

Scott was still amazed at the cartwheel. "That's pretty amazing, peanut." Then his own phone rang. He looked at the screen. "Sorry. It's work."

He met Luis in the parking lot of a little strip mall and could tell Luis was dying to start talking. Before he let him get carried away, Scott said, "Just give me the facts. Just the facts, only the facts. Breathe. Focus. Keep it simple."

"No, no, no. No doubt, no doubt," Luis said, and then he started in like Scott hadn't said anything at all.

"Okay, so I'm at this art museum with my cousin Ignacio, right? And there was this, like, abstract expressionism exhibit, and you know me, I'm more like a neo-cubist kind of guy, right? But there was this one Rothko that was sublime, bro, oh my God—"

"Luis."

"Okay, sorry, I'm just . . . you know, uh, I just get excited and stuff. But anyway, anyway. Ignacio tells me, 'Yo, I met this crazy-fine writer chick at the spot last night, like, fine,

fine, crazy-stupid fine.' So this writer chick tells Ignacio, 'Yo, I'm like a boss in the world of guerrilla journalism, and I got mad connects with the peeps behind the curtains, y'know what I'm sayin'?' Ignacio's like, 'For real?' And she's like, 'Yeah. You know what, I can't tell you who my contact is, because he works with the Avengers.'"

"Oh no," Scott said.

"Yeah. Like he comes up to him and he says, y'know, 'I'm looking for this dude who's most unseen, who's flashing this fresh tech, who's got, like, bomb moves, right? Who you got?' And she's like, 'Well, we got everything nowadays. We got a guy who jumps, we got a guy who swings, we got a guy who crawls up the walls, you gotta be more specific.'

"And he's like, 'I'm looking for a guy who shrinks.'

"I got all nervous 'cause I keep mad secrets for you, bro. So I asked Ignacio, 'Did he tell the stupid-fine writer chick to tell you to tell me because I'm tight with that man that he's looking for him?'"

"And? What'd he say?"

Luis had never looked so excited. "He said yes."

The Avengers, Scott thought. No way. The Avengers!

Falcon was looking for him. Had to be Falcon. And he was being cool about it. If they'd just wanted to come after Scott for the job he'd pulled in upstate New York, that would have been simple. Like, Iron Man could have been waiting in Paxton's front yard anytime. But they were keeping it quiet, which meant they really wanted to talk.

Like maybe about Scott Lang being an Avenger.

No, Scott corrected himself.

They wanted Ant-Man.

TURN THE PAGE TO
SEE A SNEAK PEEK

CHAPTER 1

The twins knew something was wrong. They reached for each other and touched hands, wondering what they should do. Around them, alarms and sirens blared. They heard explosions from outside the Leviathan Chamber. Soldiers ran to take up defensive positions. Before them, the scepter stood in its housing, the blue energy from its gem crackling in the air above it.

The Avengers charged through a snowy forest toward the fortress that was their target, at the edge of the city of Sokovia. Enemy soldiers fired at them. Hawkeye located one of the soldiers' firing positions and blew it up with an explosive arrow. Thor smashed another gunner's nest with his hammer. The soldiers inside tumbled out, falling out of the tree. Hulk took on the heavy equipment, smashing a tank and looking around for another one.

Zooming overhead, Iron Man crashed hard into an invisible energy shield protecting the fortress. He swore as he tumbled to the ground.

"Language, Stark," Captain America said. "Jarvis, what's the view from upstairs?"

Jarvis was feeding information into the displays inside Iron Man's helmet. "It appears the central building is protected by some kind of energy shield. Strucker's use of alien technology is well beyond that of any other HYDRA base we've taken down."

All the other Avengers could hear him because of their communication devices on a secure team-only wavelength.

"Loki's scepter must be there," Thor said. "Strucker couldn't have mounted this defense without it. At long last…"

"At long last is lasting a little long, boys," Black Widow said.

"Yeah," Hawkeye commented from behind a tree, where he was picking off HYDRA soldiers one after another. "I think we're losing the element of surprise."

Soldiers poured out of the fortress, lining its exterior walls and counterattacking. The Avengers were closer to it now. On the other side of the fortress was the city. Iron Man soared over the fortress. He couldn't get through the energy shield protecting the main keep, but the soldiers on the walls were outside the shield. He fired repulser beams at them and dodged their return fire. Some of them had Chitauri weapons.

In the forest, racing toward the fortress, the rest of the Avengers fought Strucker's troops. Captain America skidded to a halt on his motorcycle and threw it at a jeep. The jeep swerved and crashed into a tree.

Inside the fortress, Baron Strucker strode through the command center, looking for the officer on duty. "Who gave the order to attack?"

The soldier nearest him stammered, "Herr Strucker, it's...it's the Avengers."

Another soldier, more calmly, added, "They landed in the far woods. The perimeter guard panicked."

"They have to be after the scepter," Strucker said. "Can we hold them?"

"They're the Avengers!" the first soldier said, as if he couldn't believe the question.

The Avengers, Strucker thought. *Everyone fears them.* "Deploy the rest of the tanks," he ordered a waiting officer. "Concentrate fire on the weak ones. A hit may make them close ranks." He turned to a scientist accompanying him, Dr. List. "Everything we've accomplished...we're on the verge of our greatest breakthrough!"

"Then let's show them what we've accomplished," Dr. List answered smoothly. "Send out the twins."

"It's too soon."

"It's what they signed up for," Dr. List pointed out.

Strucker shook his head, watching the soldiers deploy out of the command center. "My men can hold them," he said, but inside he wasn't sure.

CHAPTER 2

A heavy Chitauri gun fired at Iron Man. The beam missed him and destroyed part of a building in Sokovia. "Sir, the city is taking fire," Jarvis said.

"Strucker's not going to worry about civilian casualties," Tony said. "Send in the Iron Legion."

The Iron Legion was a squadron of remotely operated Iron Man armored suits. They landed in different parts of Sokovia. "Please return to your homes," one said. "We will do our best to ensure your safety during this engagement."

In another part of the city, another Iron Legionnaire broadcast its recorded speech. "This quadrant is unsafe. Please back away. We wish to avoid collateral damage and will inform you when the current conflict is resolved. We are here to help."

Not all the Sokovians loved the Avengers. One of them threw a bottle of acid at the Iron Legionnaire. It smashed on the legionnaire's mask, melting partway through it.

Tony got a damage report from the legionnaire. *What ingrates,* he thought. Then he had to dodge incoming fire and decided the legionnaires were on their own.

Strucker rallied his troops, knowing the Avengers would eventually breach the fortress's defenses. "Once again, the West bring violence to your country! Your homes! But they will learn the price of their arrogance! We will not yield. The American send their circus freaks to test us, and we will send them back in bags! No surrender!"

The men cheered as Strucker turned and spoke quietly to Dr. List. "I'm going to surrender. Delete everything. If we give the Avengers the scepter, they may not look too far into what we've been doing with it."

"But the twins," Dr. List protested.

"They're not ready to take on—"

Dr. List pointed. "No, I mean...the twins."

Strucker turned to see where Dr. List was pointing. A moment ago, the twins had been waiting, together as always, near the scepter in a shadowed corner of the room.

Now they were gone.

Hawkeye dodged the crackling blue beams of the Chitauri weapons, finding cover behind a tree. He rolled out and fired at one of the defending gunners.

The arrow disappeared. What the—?

He drew his bow again and was about to let fly when something hit him hard enough to knock him sprawling back into the trees. He got up ready to fight, and for a split second a man appeared in front of him, wearing a close-fitting blue suit, with a shock of white hair. The man held up Clint's arrow.

"You didn't see that coming?" he said mockingly. Then, before Hawkeye could respond, the man vanished.

No, not vanished. Ran at an incredible speed. For just a moment, Hawkeye had seen him start to move.

In the moment he spent thinking about that, a blast tore through his side. He spun and went down hard.

"Clint!" Black Widow called. "Clint's hit."

Captain America ran to Hawkeye's aid and was knocked hard out of the way, slamming into a tree trunk. He looked around and called out, "We've got an Enhanced in the field!" That was their term for other people like the Avengers, who had some kind of power unknown to regular humans.

Black Widow got to Hawkeye's side. "Can someone take out that bunker?" She ducked away from incoming fire.

The Hulk was the first to respond, plowing through the bunker and destroying it. "Thank you," Black Widow said. She looked down at Hawkeye's wound. It was bad.

"Stark, we really need to get inside," Captain America said. The invisible shield was holding them up, and they still didn't know where the Enhanced was or what he could do.

"I'm closing in," Iron Man said. A Chitauri beam knocked him off balance in the air. "Jarvis, am I closing in? You see a power source for that shield?"

He landed on the outside wall of the fortress, knocking soldiers away as Jarvis responded, "There's a dense particle wave below the north tower."

"Great," Iron Man said. He fired repulsors down a narrow alley, blasting open a gate. "I want to poke it with something."

Taking to the air again, he concentrated his fire on the shield in that area. A rupture appeared, and the shield began to lose coherence. The hole got larger, energy spitting around its edge. They were through!

"Drawbridge is down, people!" Iron Man called out.

Captain America heard him and turned to Thor, who was finishing off the closest defending soldiers. "The Enhanced?" Thor asked.

"He's a blur," Cap said. "All the new players we've faced, I've never seen this." He scanned the woods and the outside of the fort. "Actually, I still haven't."

"Clint's hit pretty bad, guys," Black Widow said over their comm link. "We're gonna need evac."

More tanks and soldiers started spilling from the fortress gate. "I'll get Barton to the jet," Thor said. "The sooner we're gone, the better. You and Stark secure the scepter."

"Copy that," Cap said. Soldiers charged out from their cover, with a tank coming up behind them. All of them were in a single line because of how thick the forest was in their area. "It's like they're lining up," Thor said.

Cap knew what he was getting at. "Well, they're excited," he said.

He held out his shield, and Thor swung Mjolnir against it, sending a shock wave down the path that scattered the soldiers and destroyed the tank. They'd practiced that move, and both of them grinned to see it work.

Thor began spinning his hammer, getting ready to take off. "Find the scepter!" he called.

"And for God's sake, watch your language," Iron Man added.

Cap headed for the fortress. He couldn't help but smile at Tony's joke. "That's not going away anytime soon."

CHAPTER 3

With the shield down, Iron Man could fly straight through the fortress's large windows into what looked like a command center. The soldiers inside hit him with everything they had, mostly machine guns, but they couldn't hurt the suit. "Let's talk this over," Tony said, holding up his arms...then he took every single one of them out with a burst of disabling fire from his shoulder guns. He nodded, surveying what he had done. "Good talk."

Most of the soldiers weren't in any shape to reply, but one of them groaned. "No it wasn't."

Grinning, Tony moved deeper into the fortress. He found a scientist busy at a computer terminal in another room and leveled him with a repulsor blast. Then he looked at the computer and opened the Iron Man armor to get out of it. "Sentry mode," he said. Then he pulled out a small device and set it next to the computer. It lit up and started copying all the data from the terminal. "Okay, Jarvis, you know I want it all. Make sure you copy Hill at HQ."

Outside, two legionnaires carried Hawkeye on a stretcher as Black Widow watched. "We're all locked down out here," she said. The rest of the soldiers were surrendering, with Thor making sure they didn't get any ideas about further resistance.

Captain America was going inside. "Then get to Banner," he said. "It's time for a lullaby." The Hulk was a powerful ally, but he could also be dangerous. Black Widow had the best rapport with him and was the best at getting him to turn back into Bruce Banner.

Back at the computer terminal, Tony was looking around. "He's got to be hiding more than data," he said out loud. "Jarvis, give me an IR scan." Maybe something would show up on infrared that Tony couldn't see.

"The wall to your left," Jarvis said. "I'm reading steel reinforcement... and an air current."

Tony looked more closely. There was a tiny line in the wall. He followed it with his fingertips, looking... "Please be a secret door, please be a secret door..."

With a click, the door slid aside.

"Yay," Tony said. On the other side of the doorway was a long, dark stairway. He headed down.

Black Widow found the Hulk tearing apart the remains of an enemy tank. She approached carefully and sat where he could see her. "Hey, big guy," she said. "Sun's getting real low."

The Hulk stopped what he was doing and scowled at her. She held out one hand, palm up. He hesitated, then did the same. Natasha ran her fingers softly over his palm and up the inside of his wrist. She felt the tensions simmering in every fiber of the Hulk's muscles. He sighed and pulled away from her, walking slowly—and his change started. He shrank and the green color vanished from his skin. By the time he reached the other side of the clearing from the destroyed tank, he was Bruce Banner again, staring into space as he recovered from the change. Natasha found a blanket and put it over him. She was the only Avenger who could do this. It had started to mean a lot to her. Bruce was still haunted by some of the things he'd done while he was the Hulk, and it made Natasha feel better to know that he trusted her. She waited with him and also for word from inside Baron Strucker's fortress.

Captain America punched his way through the fortress garrison until he caught Strucker trying to escape deeper into the maze of passages and rooms. "Baron Strucker," Cap said. "HYDRA's number one thug."

"Technically, I'm a thug for S.H.I.E.L.D.," Strucker said.

"Well, then, technically you're unemployed," Cap shot back. "Where's Loki's scepter?"

"Don't worry, I'll give you the precious scepter. I know when I'm beat. You'll mention how I cooperated, I hope?"

"I'll put it right under 'illegal human experimentation,'" Cap said, referring to the Enhanced they had seen outside. "How many are there?"

Strucker was looking over his shoulder, a sudden smile on his face. Cap turned to see a young woman coming out of the shadows. She was slim and alluring, but also strange, her eyes wide and not quite focused on him. There was definitely something off about her. He had just completed that thought when she flicked her wrist and sent him flying without ever touching him. He rolled down a flight of stairs, his shield absorbing some of the impact. By the time he'd gotten to his feet and raced back into the room, she was gone. A heavy vault door ground shut behind her.

"We've got a second Enhanced," he warned the team. "Female. Do not engage."

Strucker was gloating. "You're going to have to move faster than that if—"

Captain America was out of patience. He knocked Strucker into the wall and considered what to do next.

Coming out of the tunnel at the bottom of the secret staircase, Tony Stark found himself in a huge chamber littered with equipment. He was still taking it all in when Cap's voice came over the comm link. "Guys, I got Strucker."

"Yeah," Tony said. "I got...something bigger."

Suspended from the ceiling was a Chitauri Leviathan. The last time Tony had seen one of them, it had been trying to destroy New York City. He looked up at it, then got himself focused on the lab equipment again. There were prototype weapons, some robotic components, strange biotech assemblies...it would take him some time to figure out what all of it was.

And there, set into a pedestal with cables and conduits running out of it, was Loki's scepter. "Thor," Tony said into the comm. "I got eyes on the prize."

He started toward the scepter, looking closely at it to see if it was defended in some way. He was so focused on it that he never saw the woman next to him, whispering in his ear as red tendrils of magical energy wormed out from her fingertips and into his mind.

Tony turned and saw the Leviathan, whole and roaring over him. He was in an alien landscape, the sky overhead thick with stars. There were bodies everywhere, soldiers in strange uniforms...and the Avengers. Thor, Black Widow, the Hulk, Captain America. All dead. Cap was closest. Still eyeing the Leviathan, Tony knelt to see if Cap still bore any signs of life—and Cap's arm shot out! He grabbed Tony. "You could have saved us. Why? Why didn't you do more? We could have...saved..."

Cap's hand fell away, and he died.

Tony looked up and saw not one Leviathan but ten, then a hundred, surrounded by an endless fleet of alien vessels, all lifting off from this dead planet and heading for Earth, which hung like a shining blue marble in distant space...

Tony snapped out of it, dropping to his knees, sweat pouring down his face from the intensity of the vision. What had happened to him? Must have been a flashback from the Battle of New York. He looked back to the scepter. All their problems had started there, and once the Avengers had the scepter, those problems would be over. He reached out and took Loki's scepter.

From the shadows, the twins watched. "We're just going to let him take it?" the man asked quietly.

His sister nodded, a wicked smile on her face. She had a plan.

CHAPTER 4

The Avengers' Quinjet soared high into the atmosphere, headed from Sokovia back to base. Tony was in the pilot's chair. Behind him, Hawkeye lay on a chair folded down as a makeshift gurney. Thor, Black Widow, and Captain America watched over him. He was in rough shape. Behind them all, Bruce sat by himself.

Natasha went back to him, knowing she could do nothing for Clint right then. "Hey," she said. "The lullaby worked better than ever."

Bruce still looked worried. "I wasn't expecting a Code

Green." That was what they had started calling his transformations into the Hulk.

"If you hadn't been there, there would have been double the casualties. And my best friend would have been a treasured memory."

"You know, sometimes exactly what I want to hear isn't exactly what I want to hear," Bruce said.

Natasha considered this. She spent a lot of time trying to help Bruce, but sometimes she thought he didn't want to be helped. "How long before you trust me?"

He looked up at her. "It's not you I don't trust."

Their gazes met. She was really starting to care for him, and she knew he felt the same. "Thor!" she said. This would help. "Report on the Hulk?"

"The gates of Hel are filled with the screams of his victims!" Thor said proudly. She shot him a glare, and he realized his mistake. "But not the screams of the dead," he added quickly. "Wounded screams, mainly. Whimpering. A great roar of complaining, and tales of sprained, uh...deltoids. And gout."

Bruce and Natasha looked at each other again, smiling now at Thor's awkwardness.

"Banner," Tony said from the pilot's chair. "Dr. Cho's on her way from Seoul. Okay if she sets up in your lab?"

Bruce nodded. "She knows her way around."

More quietly, Tony consulted with Jarvis. "Tell her to prep everything. Barton's going to need the full treatment."

"Very good, sir," Jarvis said. "Approach vector is locked."

"Jarvis, take the wheel," Tony said. He spun in his chair and went back to Thor, who sat with the scepter wrapped in a cloth. None of them wanted to touch it bare-handed.

"Feels good, right?" Tony prompted. "You've been after this thing since S.H.I.E.L.D. collapsed. Not that I haven't enjoyed our little raiding parties, but…"

"But this brings it to a close," Thor said.

Cap joined them. "As soon as we find out what else that thing's been used for. And I don't just mean weapons. Since when is Strucker capable of human enhancement?"

"Banner and I will give it the once-over before it goes back to Asgard," Tony said. To Thor, he added, "Cool with you. Just a few days until the farewell party. You're staying, right?"

"Of course," Thor said. "A victory should be honored with revels."

"Well, hopefully this puts an end to the Chitauri and HYDRA," Cap said. "So, yes. Revels."

Around sunset the Quinjet arced over New York City and braked to a landing on the new pad on top of Avengers Tower. Tony had rebuilt the building after the Battle of New York, and it was better than ever. No longer just Stark Tower, now it was the headquarters and research center for the Avengers.

Maria Hill met them on the landing pad. As Thor and the others went with Hawkeye to the lab for his treatment, Cap and Tony stayed with Agent Hill. "Dr. Cho's all set up, boss," she said to Tony.

He nodded toward Captain America. "He's the boss. I just pay for everything, design everything, and make everyone look cooler."

"What's the word on Strucker?" Cap asked.

"NATO's got him," Hill said. The European military authorities would hold him until they decided what to do.

"And the two Enhanced?"

She handed Cap a file. He looked at it and saw two pictures, one of each of the Enhanced they had seen in the Sokovian fortress. They had been photographed at a political rally protesting American involvement in Sokovia. "Wanda and Pietro Maximoff," she said. "Twins, orphaned at ten, when a shell collapsed their apartment building. Sokovia's had a rough history. It's nowhere special, but it's on the way to everywhere special."

Cap took this in. He was more interested in people than geopolitics. "Their abilities?"

"He's got increased metabolism and improved thermal homeostasis. Her thing is neuroelectric interface. Telekinesis, mind control..."

He was looking at her the way he always did when she used specialized vocabulary.

"He's fast and she's weird," Hill said to keep it simple.

Cap nodded. "They're going to show up again."

"Agreed," Hill said. "File says they volunteered for Strucker's experiments. It's nuts."

"Yeah," Cap said. "What kind of monster lets a German scientist experiment on them to protect their country?"

He watched her get his joke. That was exactly what Steve Rogers had done during World War II. "We're not at war, Captain," Hill said.

"They are," Cap answered.

Tony got repairs started on the damaged Iron Legionnaires, checked on Hawkeye, and then met Bruce outside the lab. "How's he doing?" Bruce asked.

"Unfortunately, he's still Barton," Tony said. "He's fine. He's thirsty."

Bruce went to join Dr. Cho at Hawkeye's bedside. Tony turned his attention to the scepter, which he had put into a device specially designed to hold it for analysis. "Look alive, Jarvis. It's playtime. We've got only a couple of days with this joystick, so let's make the most of it. How we doing with the structural and compositional analysis?"

"The scepter is alien," Jarvis responded. "There are elements I can't quantify."

"So there are elements you can?"

"The jewel appears to be a protective housing for something inside," Jarvis said. "Something very powerful."

"Like a reactor?"

"Like a computer. I believe I'm deciphering code."

Huh, Tony thought. *That's a new wrinkle.* He dug into the problem and lost track of time.